Killer Holiday

Killer Holiday

By Amy Korman

Killer Holiday

Killer Punch

Killer Getaway

Killer WASPs

Killer Holiday

A Killer WASPs Mystery

AMY KORMAN

WITNESS
IMPULSE

An Imprint of HarperCollins Publishers

KILLER HOLIDAY. Copyright © 2017 by Amy Korman. All rights reserved. Printed in the United States of America. No part of this book may be used or reproduced in any manner whatsoever without written permission except in the case of brief quotations embodied in critical articles and reviews. For information, address Harper-Collins Publishers, 195 Broadway, New York, NY 10007.

Digital Edition OCTOBER 2017 ISBN: 978-0-06-243136-3
Print Edition ISBN: 978-0-06-243137-0

Cover design by Nadine Badalaty
Cover images © pink pig/Shutterstock

WITNESS logo and WITNESS IMPULSE are trademarks of HarperCollins Publishers in the United States of America.
HarperCollins is a registered trademark of HarperCollins Publishers in the United States of America and other countries.

FIRST EDITION

17 18 19 20 21 LSC 10 9 8 7 6 5 4 3 2 1

For Laura,
a beautiful star in Heaven

Chapter One

BOOTSIE MCELVOY BURST through the front door of The Striped
Awning, a bag of ice in her right hand and the biggest bottle of
Maker's Mark bourbon I've ever seen in her left. She dug into her
L.L. Bean tote for a bottle of red wine, a shaker of nutmeg, and a
bag of fun-size candy canes, all of which she deposited next to a
display of 1940s barware near the front of my antiques store.

"Kristin, it's December fifteenth, which means it's time for you
to start offering shoppers a specialty cocktail the minute they set
foot inside your store," Bootsie told me. "I'm going to mix up a
batch of the Delaney family Christmas drink, the Bourbon Blit-
zen, which never fails to produce a *White Christmas* vibe. One sip
and you'll feel like you're singing and dancing with Bing Crosby
and Danny Kaye at a snowy Vermont inn. This should double
your sales totals for the month."

"Thanks!" I said gratefully, since Bootsie's family's boozy
drinks are known throughout our village of Bryn Mawr, Pennsylvania, for their potency and tendency to produce unwise purchases.

"The drinks sound good, but you're also going to need about four thousand more of these pinecones, triple the greenery, and eight hundred additional strands of lights," Joe Delafield informed me; he'd arrived twenty minutes earlier to help me with decorating my store for the Christmas rush—though, to be honest, the holidays aren't exactly a great time of year for antiques sales.

To lure in passing foot traffic, I'd brought in armloads of holly and spruce branches from my backyard (cost: free, thankfully), spray-painted pinecones silver (the paint was only $5.28 at the hardware store), and added some cheerful-looking blinking white lights, which I thought looked very festive. This would probably bring tons of holiday shoppers through my front door!

"After that, I'd drape these chandeliers with about seventy-five yards of silver ribbon and another carload of holly branches from those overgrown shrubs at your house." Joe paused, eyeing the room with his signature critical stare. "The effect I'm going for is that a bunch of HGTV-crazed elves with subscriptions to *Veranda* magazine snuck in and decorated for four straight days. Gerda, we're going to need the blinking lights to stop blinking, pronto. Pull the plug, please."

Joe's assistant for the day was the eponymous owner of Gerda's Bust Your Ass Gym, which is housed inside the beauty salon across the street. Since Gerda stands a lofty six feet tall in flats (or sneakers, which is her usual footwear, since fancy shoes aren't her style), she'd agreed to hang lights and ornaments, bringing her signature grim attitude to the proceedings.

"Cute idea," Bootsie observed, casting a dubious stare at my front window, which was filled with antique silver-plated candlesticks, flatware, and wineglasses. "Is that your holiday inventory?"

I'd tied festive red ribbons around the candlesticks and wineglass stems, but even I had to admit that my gift ideas had limited appeal. I nodded, sighing. I'd been thinking of adding gift-y dog treats, but my own hound, Waffles, can vault himself into the front window area, and I knew from past experience that he'd eat the whole display the minute I turned my back. As if realizing I was thinking about him, he gave me a happy little wag from his dog bed up in the front of the store.

"Nobody going to want that stuff," said Gerda, who moved here from her native Austria a few years back. Gerda, who's incredibly muscular and brings in sell-out crowds at her Pilates classes, isn't the most tactful person in the world. "People want, like, scarves and Fitbits and iPhones."

I sighed, knowing Gerda was right. Those *were* the gifts on most holiday wish lists.

"Luckily, I've solved all your problems," Bootsie told me. "I ran into Eddie from the Pub this morning, and he needs a place to hold some late-night poker tournaments this month, so I brokered a deal for The Striped Awning. You'll be hosting twice-weekly games from 10 p.m. till 1 a.m., Tuesdays and Thursdays till Valentine's Day."

"What!" I erupted, alarmed by this idea. "First of all, that doesn't sound legal."

"It's fine," she told me, waving away my concerns. "I mean, it's not like it will be a professional betting operation. Eddie's limiting each night to ten players and three hours. Some cards, a few drinks, a few small wagers. What could go wrong?"

"A lot!" I said. "They'll blow cigar smoke and drop Dorito crumbs everywhere. Not to mention get arrested for operating a casino without a license. A *lot* could go wrong!"

"You worry too much," Bootsie informed me dismissively. "Plus, he'll pay you two hundred dollars a night to use the store."

I opened my mouth to respond, but no words came out. Bootsie knew she had me—there's no way I can refuse an extra four hundred dollars a week, even if it puts me on the wrong side of the state gaming commission. Bootsie started to brag about how if she was running The Striped Awning, there would be pop-up Lilly Pulitzer and Lands' End kiosks beginning in late November—and have the irresistible scent of Pillsbury Cinnamon Rolls wafting out onto the sidewalk to lure in customers (which actually sounded like a good idea).

Just then, though, the front door was thrown open by one Sophie Shields, a tiny blonde who at the moment was looking slightly wild-eyed.

"Ya won't believe what just happened!" shrieked Sophie. "The Colketts were helping me put up curtains in my new dining room, since Joe here never finished decorating my place—*and* the curtains are orange silk, by the way, they're totally *Elle Decor* meets a J. Lo red-carpet gown. So Tim and Tom Colkett were talking paint colors when I heard a horn honking, so I opened the front door, thinking it was the delivery boy from the Hoagie House. We were all starving and we'd ordered a couple of turkey subs, so I figured I'd go out and pay the driver, when *boom!*

"A guy dressed as Santa leaned out of the driver's seat of a black SUV that had pulled right up in my driveway and aimed a gun at me and the Colketts!" The Colketts are the town's leading landscape designers, who've lately turned their talents to party planning and interior design, thereby irritating Joe, who's a professional decorator and doesn't like the competition.

"Then the guy yelled, 'Hey, Sophie, this one's from your ex, Barclay!' and shot my favorite handbag!" Sophie finished. "I was reaching into it to pay for the hoagies, thank goodness, so it acted as a protective shield. Also, I think maybe this Santa guy doesn't have great aim."

We all stared at her for a moment.

"Are you sure, Sophie?" said Bootsie finally. "Because this sounds like BS."

"Yeah, Sophie, maybe you been hitting the wine bottle today," seconded Gerda. "I know the Colketts are day drinkers. Maybe you been guzzling alcohol, too."

"It's true!" Sophie bleated. "Just look at this Ferragamo satchel! If it hadn't had gold hardware to block the trajectory of the bullet, me and the Colketts would have been toast!"

She held up a beautiful and pricey-looking purse, from which emanated a faint whiff of smoke. One side of the handbag was in shreds, and the gold buckle was dented from impact. Gerda took the handbag, opening it up to pull out lip gloss, a wad of twenties, a giant pair of sunglasses, and, finally, a dinged-up bullet.

"Sophie," said Gerda, "I apologize. I admit I thought you were drunk and made this whole story up. Did you call police?"

"I don't need the police, since the evil Santa told me it was my ex who sent him. I'm calling my lawyers!" fumed Sophie.

She was speed-dialing her legal team (for about the millionth time, since Sophie's divorce from a former midlevel mafia exec is going into its third year of negotiations over things like missing shrimp forks, and who gets to sit at Table 11 at Restaurant Gianni, the town's best Italian spot) when the door of The Striped Awning opened, and we heard another familiar voice that didn't contribute to the jolly holiday vibe.

"I'm back from the first leg of my round-the-world cruise!" sang out Eula Morris, our high school nemesis and all-around annoying girl who likes to boss people around.

Chapter Two

I'D BEEN LOOKING forward to a peaceful, eggnog-scented Yuletide season this year, one bedecked with swags of fresh greenery, filled with crackling logs and holiday movie binge-watches. This year, I'd thought hopefully, Joe and our friend Holly Jones wouldn't have their annual fight about whether wrapping paper "color themes," and Sophie and Joe would forgo arguments about whether her blinding decorations on every single tree in her yard was "Vegas-Miami bling-tastic!" (her opinion) or "something the town zoning committee should shut down" (his take on it).

Sure, there would be Bootsie's family's boozy annual holiday party, where you're forced to do sing-alongs and there's an outdoor bonfire in weather that's absolutely freezing (the Delaneys and McElvoys all wear about seventeen layers of L.L. Bean clothes and never get cold). And there's the inevitable problem with the New Year's Day brunch, because none of us except Joe can cook, and once he starts drinking, no one knows if the traditional ham is done, or how long to bake a broccoli quiche.

Plus, only Joe and Bootsie like ham. But these are all minor holiday misunderstandings—plus, we've been eating spiral ham now for ten years, and it doesn't seem like any of us is suddenly going to start basting, say, a roast beef.

Anyway, the holiday season had kicked off with one of those perfect Thanksgivings where everything goes right: Holly and her husband, Howard, had hired the Bryn Mawr Country Club staff to cook an amazing meal. Bootsie, who spends ninety-five percent of her time on her *Bryn Mawr Gazette* job and on the tennis court, actually decided to devote the day to family, and brought her ever-patient husband, Will; their adorable sons; her parents the Delaneys; and her brother, Chip, to the festive gathering. Sophie and Joe held hands at the table and refrained from bickering, with Sophie proudly wearing the pre-engagement ring Joe had given her last summer and Joe only making two comments about Sophie's gold Gucci boots being seen from space (these metallic boots looked good on her, honestly, and gave the whole day a little extra oomph).

My own handsome, loyal, and good-hearted boyfriend, local veterinarian John Hall, had made it through the entire meal without a single cow or goat needing a house call. Even Gerda had been in a good mood, limiting her dire warnings about how an American harvest holiday had

somehow become a gravy gravy-and become a gravy-and-stuffing-fest that did permanent damage to arteries and would be better celebrated with a Tofurky and a healthfully prepared puree of pumpkin that included no butter, salt, sugar, or flour.

But then on December 1, Sophie's lawyers had told her that they were finally days away from having papers she could sign that would officially end her marriage to her ex Barclay Shields, that former mafia exec who she'd been separated from for some three years.

Most important of all, she would be free to marry again!

Sophie had gone into a *Brides*-magazine-fueled meltdown and told Joe she was "over" summer weddings with gorgeous tents full of lush roses and balmy, breezy temperatures, plus she'd read in *Town & Country* that winter was the new wedding season, and what about New Year's Day, which was just thirty-one short days away—and would make for totally romantic nuptials!

Because she'd checked, and they could rent out Restaurant Gianni, and have an amazing all-white decor with just-made pastas, fresh ricotta pizzas, and Umbrian wines, and probably get some guys she knew from Atlantic City to do the music from *Jersey Boys* plus some classic disco hits, and in case Joe didn't know, Angelina Jolie had worn Versace for her wedding to Brad. Also, the *Bryn Mawr Gazette*'s annual wedding guide was coming up, and was interested in covering their nuptials.

Joe told Sophie he was busy on New Year's Day making his famous maple-bourbon glaze for the traditional ham, and liked to both watch football and plan new paint colors that afternoon, so that day wouldn't work. When they got to discussing the honeymoon, Sophie voted for flying nonstop to Venice and bringing an empty suitcase to tote home full of new shoes, and then spending two weeks in Miami where she could easily ship home additional handbags, sunglasses, and makeup.

Joe said he hoped Sophie would have fun, because he'd be staying at a peaceful inn while antiques hunting in Provence, or renting a cottage in rural Connecticut, which Sophie said sounded like something only someone toting an AARP card or a guy who didn't know how to have fun would do on a post-wedding jaunt.

Things had exploded after that, and the next day, Sophie had

FedExed the pre-engagement ring back to Joe at Holly's house, where he had taken up residence after his Sophie blowup.

To fill the void left by Sophie, Joe had since signed on to a new part-time gig in Florida renovating an adorable fishing cottage owned by one Adelia Earle, a feisty tobacco heiress he frequently works for, and was now knee-deep in pink and green fabrics half of each month. This wasn't improving his mood, since Adelia changes her mind fairly often, and requires tons of meetings about things like pompom trim on cushions.

Also on the downside, business was a little slow at The Striped Awning, and I was still trying to figure out the perfect gift for John. I'd been knitting sweaters for both him and Waffles. The one for Waffles, which was basically a scarf sewed into a basset-shaped funnel, was going quite a bit better.

However, happily, the weather was a relatively balmy forty-seven degrees in December, which was great, because my heater doesn't work all that well. And heating bills are expensive!

Anyway, our town being quite small, and given that Sophie and Joe were bound to run into each other about nineteen times a week on the street, in the luncheonette, at the Pack-N-Ship, and at the Bryn Mawr Pub, the former couple had agreed they were just going to pretend the other one didn't exist. Anyway, judging by the sad, longing glances Joe and Sophie frequently exchanged, I still had hope they'd work things out.

Plus, on a happier note, the whole town was getting into holiday mode! There were cute, colorful lights over the door into the luncheonette, and a funky all-white Christmas tree made from fake feathers visible through the window of Le Spa.

As I looked around at the layers of holly and silver ribbon and inhaled the scent of the bourbon Bootsie was liberally glugging into a huge pitcher for a test batch of her themed cocktail, something akin to holiday excitement started to well up inside me, and I could practically hear the strains of "Jingle Bells" wafting around town square, just outside The Striped Awning.

Oh, wait—I *did* hear "Jingle Bells," I realized—the Bryn Mawr Town Singers were warming up their vocal cords for a practice session for the town holiday festivities next week.

However, the return of Eula Morris didn't add to the merry vibe.

"Hi, Eula," said Bootsie in a friendly enough manner. She and Eula share a hyper-competitive streak on the tennis court, and get along well. But for Holly and Joe, Eula was truly the Nightmare Before Christmas, and the Abominable Snowman, Heat Miser, and Burgermeister Meisterburger all rolled into one tiny package.

It's not that Eula is pure evil, but she does tend to take over any committee or event, and run it in a less-than-flexible style. Even more irritating, Eula's usually good at the volunteer gigs she takes on, being super-organized and a good planner. But when Eula takes over a local event, including last summer's Bryn Mawr Tomato Show, which she cochaired with Holly, everyone involved usually quits.

Things didn't go exactly smoothly as Eula and Holly struggled to agree on the best way to create a stylish celebration of the glossy red salad ingredient. Since Holly is heir to a poultry fortune and her husband runs a trucking conglomerate, she ended up hiring the Colketts to turn the tomato shindig into something along the lines of the *Vanity Fair* Oscar party, but starring nightshade vegetables. Eula obviously didn't approve of the crazy soiree, but had to suck it up, because Holly paid for it.

Finally, Holly and Joe were so desperate to get rid of Eula that they'd bought twenty dollars' worth of Powerball tickets and anonymously left them in Eula's mailbox. A week later, Eula had been one of five winners of the mega-jackpot, and their plan had come to fruition.

Eula, now worth millions, had immediately embarked on her lifelong dream of sailing around the world. In September, she'd boarded a cruise ship called the *Palace of the Seas* for a twenty-four-month voyage, and our town had been blissfully Eula-free for a glorious autumn season.

"Nice tan," Bootsie added, observing the glowy hue of Eula's skin, which did look as if she'd been spending plenty of time tanning on the poop deck over the past four months.

"And I like your hair!" said Sophie. "Ya look a lot better since you hit the jackpot," she added to Eula, who gave her a happy little nod.

It was true that Eula was looking good: This bossy and competitive girl now had kicky blond highlights, wore a cute, belted down jacket, and appeared to have been taking all the Zumba and Pilates classes on her mega-ship, since she looked super-fit underneath her cool skinny corduroys.

The stylish new version of Eula was kind of a shocker—though in her midthirties, she's always dressed like she's about sixty-five years old. Of course, given my Old Navy–Gap Outlet clothing budget, I'm in no place to criticize Eula's usual lack of style. Anyway, the all-new Eula had the breezy, cute look of one of those girls who'd never worn makeup before but had just gotten one of those *Today Show* makeovers from Hoda and Kathie Lee.

"How's that boat trip going, anyway?" said Joe, looking hopeful that the ship would run into an iceberg soon, and Eula would have to float to shore clinging to a wooden door. For some reason, Joe hates Eula almost as much as Holly does. I've never completely understood the depth of his pissiness toward her, but a key stumbling block was our high school prom, which Eula tried to take over with a fifties sock-hop idea. Words like "sock hop" enrage Joe. Also, Eula is an amateur painter of fruits and vegetables in the style of Cezanne, which seems like a pleasant hobby to me, but which makes Joe angry.

"It's going amazing!" said Eula. "The crew waits on me hand and foot, and I've met everyone from deposed Russian royalty to a musician who models part-time for Armani. I also met an incredibly handsome guy who's a retired lawyer and who I've been exclusively dating for twelve weeks, and there are disco parties every night, and I've lost five pounds since I stopped going to every meal except the 11 a.m. smoothie buffet and dinner!"

"I've heard smoothies can turn your skin green over time," Joe told her. "I think I see a tinge of kale in your complexion already."

"What happened that you're back here—the boat docks for Christmas?" asked Sophie.

"Yeah, the crew wants to see their families," Eula said sourly, as if this was totally unreasonable, "so we're on dry land till December twenty-fifth. Then we take off again and spend New Year's Eve doing a moonlight limbo in Barbados!"

A small volt of jealousy surged through me, and Joe looked like he'd just been gripped by a horrible case of acid reflux. I've honestly never even considered what it would be like to float around the Caribbean and across the Atlantic toward Venice, or wherever Eula's next stop was after she'd hit every island south of Cuba, but her trip did sound kind of awesome.

Probably it was best that Holly wasn't here to listen to Eula, who was still rattling off enviable details of ports of call from Antigua to Montego Bay, and days spent kayaking around deserted islands, enjoying beach picnics, foot scrubs, and lunches of just-caught crab cocktail. Holly could afford to book herself on a similarly swanky boat trip, but who actually does that? The fact that Eula was actually sailing the seven seas in a luxury cabin with eight-hundred-thread-count sheets and a butler would inevitably be a thorn in Holly's side.

"There *is* one small problem," Eula said, aiming a sad glance at Bootsie and me and temporarily abandoning her PR campaign about how great every waking moment was on board the *Palace of the Seas*. "I got home last night, went to dinner at Restaurant Gianni with my wonderful new boyfriend, and when I got home, my suitcase was missing."

She paused for a moment, doing an awkward little foot shuffle. "And, um, I know you've solved a few little mini-crimes in town, so I thought you could figure out where my luggage has wandered off to!"

"We've got issues here already," Bootsie told her, "starting with Sophie's drive-by shooting this morning. And, I mean, you won the Powerball, so can't you just buy another suitcase? This doesn't sound like you need to alert the authorities, or our town's one police officer, the esteemed Walt. Or even his intern, Jared."

I refrained from mentioning that Jared only worked three hours a week at the police station these days. This industrious nineteen-year-old actually holds down a number of part-time gigs around town, helping out at the country club, the Pack-N-Ship, and (when he can borrow his parents' brand-new Yukon), he's also a newly minted Uber driver.

"It's a little more complicated than that," Eula told her. "And I'm going to need you to agree not to write about this in the *Bryn Mawr Gazette*, because there's a slightly sticky issue with the suitcase, which by the way is a Samsonite Black Label. That's their new upscale line of hard-sided rolling luggage, and is the newest thing in chic yet practical luxury travel," she bragged.

As the words "chic yet practical" flew forth from Eula's lips (which, I noticed, wore a very cool shade of glossy lipstick, possibly acquired in a duty-free cosmetics shop), Joe lost his grip on a giant roll of silver ribbon and almost fell off his stepladder, while Bootsie's eyes blazed angrily at the mention of the local newspaper. Bootsie's column covers real estate transactions, local charity events, and other gossipy news for the *Gazette*, and she's quite skilled at turning even the smallest event in town into a front-page story. This can be really helpful, since she'd probably feature The Striped Awning's free Bourbon Blitzens as a newsy item this week, I thought gratefully, bringing in at least a few customers who like free drinks (and who doesn't?).

But right before Eula's Powerball windfall, she'd also briefly written for the *Gazette*, and Bootsie hadn't been too happy about having her stories stolen from her.

"Plus," said Eula, "this isn't really news—it's just a teeny-weeny rollerboard suitcase gone missing. And, um, I can't report it to the police because there's one slightly illegal part of the situation."

"I'm a reporter!" Bootsie told Eula. "I've got a professional obligation to share important findings and events. That's my life! My reason for roaming this planet!"

"You write about parties and real estate," Eula told her. "And your reasons for living are drinking and playing tennis."

These two things do take up most of Bootsie's day. She also has Will and her toddlers, plus some cute yellow Labs, but to be honest, I think they see less of Bootsie than the country club, the tennis courts, and the Pub do.

"I enjoy the occasional foray into alcohol and tennis, and what's wrong with that? Anyway, I can give you a couple days off from telling my editor about the suitcase theft, but after that, I'm free to report it," Bootsie said. "That's the only deal I'm willing to make."

"Just so ya know, I *want* ya to write about Santa shooting at me and the Colketts!" Sophie interrupted, poking Bootsie in the shoulder. "And you," she said, pointing at Joe, "should feel real bad that first you trampled and stomped my heart into a pulp, and now I've got Santa after me with a gun!"

"I'll do a story on the handbag incident," Bootsie agreed. "I think the folks at Ferragamo would love to know that their bags are well-made enough to stop a bullet, and we can Instagram and Snapchat about this with all the appropriate hashtags and emojis. My editor loves that kind of cross-promotion.

"Anyway, Eula, I can agree to a one-week news embargo, but that's it. And I'm only saying that because I know this suitcase snatch must be a major fuckup for you to have to come and ask us for help. I need details, pronto!"

Chapter Three

BOOTSIE AND EULA negotiated for a few minutes, with Eula finally caving and saying a week would be a sufficient shutdown on a story about her theft, since she'd be back on the *Palace of the Seas* by Christmas, and people weren't as gossipy on the boat as they were here, *and* she had a whole new life and group of friends that were all super-interesting and international.

"So what's the big deal with your Samsonite?" demanded Sophie. "Because that's great about your new life and all, but I joined the Bryn Mawr Singers, and I've got practice in five minutes."

"Well, what happened was, the ship stopped in Paradise Island and I went a little nuts at the duty-free jewelry shops, and I also felt like I wasn't diversifying my investments enough, so I bought a few, um, gold bars. They fit right in my suitcase."

"Uh-huh, I hear you," said Bootsie, nodding as if this sort of purchase was as commonplace as the rest of us heading to Target for a few boxes of Triscuits.

"How many gold bars?" demanded Gerda.

"Oh, about eight," said Eula airily. "And when I got off the boat yesterday, the customs line was really long and I was in a hurry, so I didn't declare most of what I bought in the Bahamas.

"I said I got a sarong and a pair of wedge sandals. Which I did!" Eula added hastily. "But I didn't have time to go through explaining the gold bars, because when you have to fill out the forms for stuff like that, they charge you a bunch of taxes, plus customs takes forever!"

"Understandable," said Bootsie, who also likes to skip lines and flout laws, though not usually while carrying a Samsonite full of precious metal.

"So last night," continued Eula, "I got home and went out to dinner at Ristorante Gianni with that fantastic guy I met on the ship—he's such a gentleman—and when I got home, the suitcase was gone!"

"Let me get this straight," Joe said, after a brief detour to the bottle of Maker's Mark. "You want us to help you find a missing suitcase full of gold that you didn't declare at customs. And I would do that why? Because to put this in terms that are easy for you to comprehend, I hate you."

"I don't hate Eula," pointed out Bootsie. "We share a passion for sports and growing tomatoes."

Eula aimed a grateful glance at Bootsie, while I stayed neutral. I don't loathe Eula, but I don't exactly love her.

"You seem real annoying, but you pretty good at tennis," offered Gerda, who'd competed against Eula in a country club match the previous summer.

"To get back to my original point, why exactly would I help you?" asked Joe.

"Because I hear that you're stuck doing a renovation with an elderly lady in Florida who drives you crazy just to pay the bills, and 'cause your girlfriend dumped you and you have nothing else to do," said Eula, scoring a couple of valid points at Joe.

"And, if you get my suitcase back, I'll give the four of you one of the gold bars, which I paid thirty-nine thousand dollars each for," Eula told him. "Split that four ways between you, Kristin, Gerda, and Bootsie—I'm leaving you out, Sophie, because you don't need the money—and that's a cool nine thousand, seven hundred fifty dollars for each of you."

"Well, this has been fun, but I can see the Colketts are outside, too—they're also in the Bryn Mawr Singers—and they brought Starbucks for everyone to warm up our pipes for rehearsal," said Sophie. "See you all later," she added in our direction, pointedly ignoring Joe, who climbed back onto his ladder, sticking with his decorating duties. "Except for you!" she told him. "I don't want to see you later."

As it happened, December 15 is the day that preparations begin each year for the town square's Christmas festivities. The singers were already lined up over by the old gazebo, having a quick meeting about song selection, with Leena who owns the Pack-N-Ship, Skipper and Abby from the country club, and Bootsie's mom, Kitty Delaney, among the crooners.

"We will walk you over to this singing activity," said Gerda. "Need some fresh air after that girl's longwinded story," she stage-whispered, as Eula waved good-bye and climbed into a fancy new car.

Sophie, Bootsie, and I were halfway across the green that forms the center of the village and heading for where the singers had gathered under a little pergola when all of a sudden, Sophie—who's been uncharacteristically sad since her breakup with Joe, even with her new orange silk curtains and after her "research" trips to Vegas and Miami for her tree-decorating project in her front yard—did a little scamper-style dance and broke into a jazzy Christmas tune.

"*Sleigh bells bling, are ya glistenin'?*" she piped up in a pleasant, on-pitch voice that was surprisingly big and full, considering it was emanating from a tiny girl in five-inch heels.

"*In the lane, something, something . . .*" she sang.

With this, Sophie paused her impromptu rendition of "Winter Wonderland," and her face fell.

"This holiday is terrible!" she cried. "I don't know this song, and I don't have my Honey Bunny!" she wailed.

"I am pretty sure you got a lot of lyrics wrong," Gerda told her unsympathetically.

"Sophie, you can sing!" Bootsie erupted, stopping short in her Lands' End boots and voicing what I was thinking. "You actually sound really good!"

"Thanks!" Sophie said, cheering up slightly. "I used to be pretty good at singing. I was Sandy when we did *Grease* in high school."

"Anyone seen Chip Delaney?" screamed Leena from her post with the singers. "He's supposed to be here at practice."

"*We wish ya a Merry Christmas!*" belted out Sophie as the chorus behind her hummed a jazzy background tune. "*Good tidings for Christmas, and a happy new year!*"

Joe stuck his head out of the front door of The Striped Awning to listen, his expression mingling both surprise and heartbreak. Just then, as Sophie wound up to a big finish and onlookers broke out into cheers and applause, a Jeep pulled up by the luncheonette, and an incredibly handsome guy in his late twenties got out.

It was Channing, a former sous-chef for Gianni Brunello, our town's celebrity restaurateur who'd recently gotten his own Food Network gig, *The Angry Chef*, by way of opening a restaurant out in L.A. Channing has great cheekbones, blue eyes, wavy brown hair, and wore a chef's jacket and jeans, and had a deep tan that made his muscles look even bulgier.

The younger chef had carried on a steamy affair with Gianni's then-girlfriend Jessica a little over a year ago, and the two had fled to Florida to open their own restaurant, a cool Italian spot named Vicino.

Vicino had been such a success that Channing and Jessica had recently sold it to a group of Miami investors, and agreed to run Restaurant Gianni again for the winter while they figured out their next move. I'd been surprised that Gianni, a certified rage-aholic, had offered his ex and her boyfriend jobs, but then again, Gianni loves money more than anything else, and "Chessica" knows how to run a successful eatery. Somewhat annoyingly, the duo were even better-looking since they'd returned from living in beachy splendor down south, and retained a bronzed glow even in forty-degree weather.

"Sophie, I heard the end of your song. You sound great!" said Channing.

"Thanks, you gorgeous hunk of man!" said Sophie. "The chorus here has been real nice letting me do a couple of numbers with them. It's always been a dream of mine to be a professional singer!"

"Channing, has anyone ever told you that you look like a long-lost member of the Hemsworth family of hot Australian actors?" interrupted Bootsie, who frequently mentions the genetically blessed pasta genius as someone she'd like to jump into a hot tub with. Actually, everyone in town feels the same way, but Bootsie's not that good at subtlety.

"You're better than a Hemsworth!" added Sophie. "They wish they had your pecs and biceps!"

"Thanks!" said Channing, looking embarrassed. "You know what, Sophie? You should do some holiday songs at Ristorante Gianni. We could have a cabaret in the bar and call it, I don't know, 'One Very Merry Night Starring Sophie Shields!'"

"This sounds awesome!" shrieked Sophie. "I'm picturing Gaga-meets-Mariah as my style inspo, which means glitter and sheer gowns with strategically placed beading. How's Friday for my big opening night?"

"Perfect," Channing told her. "Probably we should get you a backup band, too."

"Huh," mused Sophie. "I don't know a band! I could ask around, or put an ad in the paper."

"I will put out a message asking for musicians on Twitter," announced Gerda. "I just joined this form of instant worldwide communication." She tapped on her phone for a second. "Tweet is sent! Now the world can tweet me auditions for Sophie's musicians."

Sophie and the Colketts started doing throaty octave warm-ups with the other dozen town singers, and I reluctantly turned around to the store. Stars were popping out in the sky above, and a big full moon had risen in the now navy-blue sky.

It was already after 5 p.m., and I had to feed Waffles, change, and be at my new part-time job at the Bryn Mawr Pub in less than twenty minutes. Waffles and I did a quick stroll in the backyard when we got home after he hoovered up his nightly kibbles, and I turned on some Christmas music as he jumped onto the couch for his after-dinner nap. I threw on my new Pub uniform—jeans and a long-sleeve T-shirt featuring an image of the bar's neon sign—and sighed as I layered on some mascara, finally giving up amid a small surge of self-pity at having to work on a Wednesday night during the holidays. Still, though, I told myself, I was lucky to have the opportunity to make the extra cash. January was fast approaching, and is the absolute slowest month of the year at The Striped Awning.

Eddie from the Pub had promised me I'd clear over seventy-five dollars a night at the Pub as a bartending assistant, and last week, I had indeed left with almost that many crumpled ones and fives at the end of my shift. And first thing in the new year, I decided, I'd finally sell all my leftover inventory on eBay! I'd make more money this January than ever before!

With that happy thought, I gave Waffles a hug and headed out to the Pub.

Chapter Four

WING NIGHT IS one of those local institutions that draws a crowd in summer, winter, and basically any night there's sports on TV or people want to drink beer.

Joe, for one, was perched gloomily on a bar stool digging into an order of salt and vinegar-soaked drumettes, while around him other patrons were munching on Caribbean jerk, teriyaki, and habanero-infused poultry.

Unfortunately, every wing variety stung the eyes, and was nearly impossible to shower off a spicy, chicken-y aroma after a shift behind the bar. Last week, Toby, a sheepdog belonging to my neighbors the Binghams, had showed up at my back door, whining and scratching for wings, even after I'd washed my hair and jumped into the tub.

Also, I was nervous about the job. While you'd think serving wings would be self-explanatory, the Pub has ten different varieties of deep-fried poultry. Eddie the owner had gone all over the state, plus made some road trips to the Jersey Shore, New York City, and a Wing Convention in Annapolis during the past year, and had added some cool new marinades with international flavors, including Thai-curry and Mexican chili rub. Different dipping sauces went with each of the new flavors, which made things complicated. It wasn't just blue cheese dressing.

On the plus side, most of the customers at the Pub drink a ton of beer, and are a kindly group. Eddie himself is pretty easygoing, too, and the job was a distraction from another subject I didn't really want to think about. Which was that my boyfriend, town vet John Hall, was out of town. Again. And at the holidays!

Even Eula Morris has a Yuletide romance, I thought in a burst of self-pity as I served baskets of hot wings to a group of guys from the firehouse. Sure, Eula was missing a bunch of gold bars, but I was missing a boyfriend, gone for the Christmas season on a business trip. I'd tried to be upbeat about his temporary absence, but was honestly feeling more miserable than merry this December.

Just then, Holly showed up at the Pub.

Maybe Holly had heard that Eula was back in town, I thought. Holly *looked* as perfect as ever to the casual observer. But I've known her since high school, and I could see past the glossy blond hair and the fabulous beige cashmere wrap sweater and the cool ankle boots to notice that her left eyelid was twitching. Also, Holly doesn't come to Wing Night.

"I have what I'd call a fairly major Christmas crisis," she told me and Joe, sliding onto a bar stool. "First of all, you know I gave Gerda a part-time job at Maison de Booze, and she's being kind of inflexible with shoppers. I mean, if someone wants to guzzle pricey cabernet during our free twice-weekly tastings but only buy a bottle of seven-dollar merlot, she can't call them 'cheapos' and tell them to leave the store. It turns out that customer service isn't Gerda's strong suit."

Holly had owned Maison de Booze, a cute and tiny garden shop–turned–wine store, since last summer, which was fun for her, since she likes gathering the town for free pinot and cheese and doesn't take the profit margin too seriously. However, adding Gerda to the staff had made things a lot more strict at the store.

"Also, someone broke into the Man Shed we were going to surprise Howard with on December twenty-fifth and took the most important item in there," she informed Joe. "They left the leather couches, the flat-screen TVs, the humidor, and the complete bound sets of *Golf Digest* and *Cigar Aficionado*. But they did steal the amazing gift that just got delivered: an amazing home distillery that whips up gallons of homemade grain alcohol in only forty-eight hours!"

Joe looked alarmed. "The thieves took the *moonshine still*? The most inspired, cool, manly holiday gift we've ever thought up for Howard? And, the one that Jared and I spent seventeen hours assembling?"

It was loud in the Pub, but had Joe just mentioned a clandestine distillery housed in Holly's former toolshed? I'd seen this kind of shack-turned-still in the movies, but never once had it turned out well for bootleggers.

People who made contraband booze always got arrested, killed, or kidnapped in a shack in the Appalachian mountains and held hostage until they turned over their entire operation to gangsters. Bootsie and I had once watched the movie *Lawless*, where we learned that simmering batches of illegal alcohol can be dangerous both in the making and the selling phases.

"Moonshiners always blow themselves up!" I warned my friends. "Or get shot about seventy-five times by rival booze makers!"

"Homemade whiskey is the latest thing in boho chic," Holly

informed me. "Everyone in Brooklyn and downtown L.A. has their own home brew, and Joe and I don't want Howard to feel like golf is his only hobby. However, it's true that the apparatus, which we ordered from a Web site operated by some guys in Kentucky, can explode."

"I would have thought your real problem would be Eula Morris coming back to town," Bootsie told Holly as she blew into the bar with Gerda on her heels. Bootsie grabbed a seat, reached for Joe's chicken wings, and started dunking one in Sriracha mayo.

I guess Holly hadn't heard the not-so-jolly news about her nemesis Eula, because she swayed on her stool and grabbed the bar for support.

Actually, Holly had appeared woozy and nauseous several times since Thanksgiving, I thought, worried. She usually sports a light tan year-round, but had been uncharacteristically pale. Also, I'd seen her order a bagel the other day at the luncheonette. Consuming solid food is out of the ordinary for Holly.

Joe was giving Holly a concerned and speculative look, too, as he politely helped her onto a bar stool.

"How about some saltines?" he suggested to Holly, taking a few packets of the deliciously bland crackers from a nearby basket on the bar top, and placing them in front of her. We all stared, openmouthed, as Holly opened one of the packets and started chewing the carb-y crackers.

Holly immediately looked less shaky, and Bootsie started telling her not only was Eula back, and that she had new blond highlights, a glowy tan, was wearing skinny corduroys, and was missing somewhere in the neighborhood of three hundred twelve thousand dollars' worth of gold bricks, when suddenly Bootsie caught sight of her brother Chip Delaney coming through the Pub's battered old front door.

"There you are!" said Bootsie angrily to Chip. "Chip, you missed practice with the singers today," she began lecturing him.

"I've got a business to run," Chip told her. "It's the holidays! People need gifts, and golf equipment is the most-requested Christmas item by men aged eighteen to seventy, and an increasing number of women, too."

Shaggy-haired and long-limbed, Chip had recently gone from working as a golf pro to opening a booming local emporium for all things greens-related, including customized clubs, jaunty clothing, and spiked shoes. His small shop had launched in early fall, and though I hadn't been inside it yet, I'd heard from Bootsie that Golf Sweet Golf was swinging along nicely.

Chip is a little older than Bootsie, but has always been young for his age, taking a few years off midcollege, and so far still living at home with his parents. Of course, Bootsie's parents are very easygoing, and their house is rambling, so Chip has his freedom.

It's impossible not to like Chip, who's built along the lines of a human Labradoodle, and is incredibly friendly. "I heard you got a Ford Super-Duty Platinum pickup," Joe said to Chip, who personally drives an Audi, but inexplicably knows a lot about cars and trucks in addition to his expertise in ikat fabrics.

"Word on the street is that your golf store is doing well," he added a bit sourly, since when Joe is miserable it's hard for him to muster up enthusiasm for other people's successes.

"Golf Sweet Golf is doing great!" agreed Chip. "And I'm working on a new business deal, too." He paused, taking on an uncharacteristically serious expression for a second. "Well, I was in on a possible new venture, but it doesn't look like it's going to work out. Anyway, the store is getting a lot of holiday traffic, so that's something."

"I read in a car magazine that the Ford Platinum series is one kickass line of truck!" said Joe. "What kind of mileage do you get on that thing?"

Chip was about to answer when all of a sudden, a guy in a leather blazer and a Shrek mask threw open the door to the Pub.

In a deep voice that carried over the Neil Diamond on the sound system, the guy boomed, "Chip Delaney. Get out here, now. Need to talk to ya. Alone."

WE STARED IN surprise as Chip walked out of the Pub. For her part, Bootsie's sky-blue eyes were bulging, and she stood frozen in place, clearly in shock. It was dark out, but Chip and his unfriendly visitor could be seen through the window to the right of the bar, each gesturing angrily as they talked.

Then, after some yelling, came a deafening bang, and Chip let out a yelp that was audible inside Wing Night. We all rushed outside to see Shrek leap into the passenger seat of a black SUV. Chip's new Ford with the Golf Sweet Golf logo had been shot in the left headlight.

"Are you okay?" screamed Bootsie, grabbing Chip.

The guy riding shotgun in the SUV tossed something long and metallic out his window into Chip's truck bed. The SUV then sped away past the luncheonette—and just visible at the wheel was a figure sporting an incongruously jolly Santa visage.

"What the hell, Chip?" demanded Bootsie. "That guy shot your truck!"

"Ohmigosh, a mob-style hit!" shrieked Sophie, who had just

pulled up behind Chip, with Gerda in tow. She jumped out of her Escalade and stared at the departing vehicle.

"Hey, that's the same Evil Santa who shot at me today!" added Sophie. "First he put a hit on my handbag, and now he pulled the trigger on Chip's truck. I know, 'cause I saw it had Jersey plates! And, the guy who came to my house today's plate also started with an S."

"It is wrong to dress up like Santa and Shrek and then commit crimes," said Gerda, following Sophie. "By the way, Chip, that Shrek guy threw a golf club into your truck and there is a note tied to it."

"Watch out!" screamed Sophie. "It could be ticking!"

"Sophie, it's a Big Bertha golf club, not a bomb," Bootsie told her, and reached into the truck bed to grab the item.

She paused to read the message, which was handwritten on plain white paper, folded up, and tethered to the golf club with some striped holiday ribbon.

"Sophie's right, Chip, this *is* some kind of mafia-style warning. It says, 'You owe us fifty grand by Monday,'" she read aloud, as Chip looked away, gulped nervously, and then started to examine the screen of his phone.

"What the hell is this about?" demanded Bootsie, grabbing Chip's elbow and giving him a noogie. I instantly flashed back to when we were fourteen and Chip had stolen Bootsie's diary, whereupon she'd tortured him for weeks with this very punishment.

"It's no big deal," hedged Chip.

"A note that says 'You owe us fifty grand' is no big deal?" said Sophie. "Not in Jersey, it isn't."

"Maybe they have the wrong guy," said Chip. "Those two probably meant to leave the note for someone else."

"It specifies you by name," Gerda told him, reaching for the golf club and reading the message for herself. "It says, '*Chip*, you owe us fifty grand by Monday.'"

Chip was reading a text on his phone, and suddenly stood up straighter, threw back his shoulders, and pulled out his car keys. He looked less Labradoodle and more determined as he got into his damaged truck and looked Bootsie squarely in the eye.

"I'll take care of this," he told his sister. "Just let me handle it."

"Wait! I'll go get Walt," said Bootsie. "I see him just across the square at the Christmas tree. The town band was rehearsing "Little Drummer Boy," which gets really loud, and Walt must not have heard the gunshot."

"Great, 'cause I need to show Walt my purse!" seconded Sophie. "Which I'm hoping my homeowners' insurance will reimburse me for, since Ferragamo ain't cheap."

A few curious faces had appeared at the Pub's window, but it seemed no one on the town square had noticed a thing: The Bryn Mawr Band was dispersing, and the town's single police officer and his intern, Jared, were completely engrossed in anchoring a ten-foot-tall blue spruce over by the pergola.

"Forget it, Bootsie. I mean it—I don't want Walt involved," said Chip.

"Why not?" demanded Bootsie, staring at Chip. "A guy shoots your truck and sends you a threatening note, and you're not going to report it?"

"Look, he could be a disgruntled shopper," Chip told her, "and you know, sometimes we say we have the lowest prices, but to be honest, you could get the same club for like, twenty dollars less at Modell's."

"That didn't look like a pissed-off golfer," offered Sophie. "It was more like a guy from Jersey who you might've screwed over in a business deal."

"Look—it's fine. I'm going to be away on business for a few days, and I don't want you freaking out or bothering me, or texting me every five seconds," Chip told Bootsie, looking her in the eye as he climbed into his damaged truck. "I'll be back by Monday after I straighten out this misunderstanding. In the meantime, leave this situation alone. See ya."

Chapter Five

"I'LL TAKE A dozen more wings," Joe told me back inside the Pub later. "And a pitcher of pilsner. Luckily, even when I'm depressed I have a great metabolism," he added dispiritedly. "Despite my breakup with Sophie, I'm still rocking a thirty-one-inch waistline."

Sophie herself had left with Gerda in tow after the Big Bertha incident, saying she needed to head home and drink a special ginger tea to coat her vocal cords, and start searching her large closet for a dress for her cabaret performance. If anything happened with Eula or Chip, we had to text her immediately, and she'd come right back to the Pub.

"How can you eat at a time like this!" Bootsie screamed at Joe, then sat down and moodily eyeballed the list of new wing flavors. "Actually, I need to keep up my strength. Let's do a couple dozen of the Thai chili ones, too."

"Have you been hitting the anxiety meds?" I asked Joe as I typed their order into the computer screen. I was concerned, since his pupils looked roughly twice their normal size. "You need to save those for later in December, when things really get stressful."

"Give me anything you have in pill form!" Bootsie demanded. "You don't know what stress is. I just watched my brother become part of a Francis Ford Coppola movie!"

"Xanax is the only way I can continue working for Adelia Earle," Joe told me, rummaging in his tote bag, emerging with a bottle of pills, and handing a tiny tablet to Bootsie, who—probably against all medical advice—downed it with her beer. "Luckily, now that Jared's an Uber driver, I can boost my booze and meds intake accordingly."

Holly gave an eye roll and ordered a plate of celery sticks, which along with the occasional grape makes up most of her daily food intake.

"How's the holiday party planning coming?" I asked Holly as I handed her the crisp green veggie and placed a wineglass in front of her. I reached under the bar for a hidden bottle of pricey cabernet, hoping to distract her from Howard's stolen gift by pouring her a glass of bordeaux from the special bottle of a fancy French vintage Eddie keeps for her and Howard at the Pub, since most wine here comes in a gallon jug. "And why aren't you in charge of the party?" I added to Joe. "I thought Holly's Christmas blowout was the highlight of your Yuletide season."

"Usually it is, and back in August I had a bunch of ideas," he agreed, "but now I'm too depressed for my best idea, which was a disco night. I told Holly to hire the Colketts to take over."

I considered this for a minute while I Windexed the bar top. Joe must *really* be down in the dumps to let the Colketts horn in on this project. Joe is über-competitive, and usually spends a fair amount of time hobnobbing at fancy events around town to land new clients.

The Pub, for instance, isn't a place Joe normally drinks away an evening, yet here he was. And allowing his best friend Holly to hire his rivals to plan a party? This was serious—Joe was in a Sophie-induced slump, which Holly was clearly worried about, too.

"You've lost your will to live, Joe. Why can't you give Sophie back her amethyst Lady Gaga ring?" Holly wondered. "Wasn't that a pre-engagement ring?"

"I tried. She keeps FedExing it back," admitted Joe.

The bauble in question was a beautiful and bling-y item that had supposedly once been worn by Sophie's favorite singer, Lady Gaga, and had mysteriously come up for sale (probably having been stolen by one of the road crew—actually the whole story sounded somewhat murky, but Joe hadn't asked too many questions of said lighting technician).

Anyway, the ring had been a big step forward for the unlikely duo.

"The amethyst bought me about four months," Joe explained, "but then Sophie told me that it was nonnegotiable that I come up with an actual engagement ring containing at least six diamonds, which could be in the form of baguettes. The bottom line is, she said if I don't propose, she's breaking things off with me for good.

"I don't like ultimatums! So that's why I'm living at your house, Holly, and even worse, that's why Gerda's back in Sophie's guest room, and I'm decorating a cottage in Florida in pink chintz and neon orange," he offered gloomily. "I should probably sign on as one of the waiters on Eula's cruise ship. At least that way I'd catch a glimpse of St. Lucia and Puerto Rico when we float by it."

"You could take the existing ring and get the Lemieuxs to replace the amethyst with a nice diamond," Holly informed him.

Here, she was referencing a shop in the next town over called Lemieux the Jeweler, known for high-end items, which is why I've never been there. It's a small, exclusive-looking spot whose exterior proclaims a quiet beauty that is quite intimidating.

"Put a rush on that rock," Holly added. "Meanwhile, the Colketts and I are way behind schedule when it comes to planning my Christmas party," Holly said, with a tragic sigh as she pushed aside her still-full glass of wine.

Holly had decided she'd host the country club's staff holiday party this year (widely known as being one of the most fun events of the year in our village, since the club's kitchen guys and waiters love to drink). As usual, planning a one-night shindig had taken up months of Holly's life.

She'd informed the club staff that she'd banned mistletoe and spruce from the party theme and was cooking up something cool and innovative, ignoring the fact that they had looked crestfallen at this bit of information.

There was no use in pointing out to Holly that people love fragrant Douglas firs, cheery strands of lights, and Elvis's *Blue Christmas* album. So the cooks and bartenders at the country club were worried, but then again, Holly's parties generally are awesome, and how bad could four hours of loud music and an open bar really be?

And the themes Holly was considering did sound promising: The Colketts had proposed a Southern Shrimp, Grits, and Crabfest. For her part, Bootsie was pushing for a soiree titled "Summer Cabin in Maine," with specialty drink tents, seats made of logs, and chili out of a can. The Colketts told Holly that both could be totally spectacular, and were constantly making notes about things like trucking in seven hundred branches of out-of-season magnolias and a dozen Bayou Classic sixty-quart aluminum pots with lid and baskets suitable for a crab boil, or building a bar entirely out of Maine-style moss, walnut branches, and fragrant spruce swags, and ordering plaid flannel shirts for fifty guests. So far, all these ideas were still under consideration by Holly, except for the flannel shirts, the thought of which had given her a cluster headache.

"And forget the themes—even the party food is a major problem. I can't ask the club staff to cater their own party. And other than this place"—she gestured around the Pub—"and Restaurant Gianni, which both close down for Christmas week, the only other restaurants in town are the luncheonette, which doesn't make food after 3 p.m., and the Hoagie House, which only has three employees."

"You could get six-foot turkey subs from there for the party," I suggested. "Everyone likes giant sandwiches!"

"I don't think turkey and Swiss is going to cut it for a fifty-person holiday party that the Colketts are flying in a forest of magnolia trees for," Holly told me.

"I just texted Chip four times with no response," Bootsie informed us. "This is scary. Maybe I *should* call Officer Walt."

Privately, I thought Bootsie had good reason to call in the police to help Chip, and was about to tell her so when Joe brushed off Bootsie's concerns about her brother.

"Chip's fine! You think that's a problem? Try renovating a house with Adelia Earle," Joe informed her. "At this point I'm drinking almost as many margaritas as she is, and I can't keep up with her. She's had years of practice."

Joe told us that Adelia's love of color made the job fun, but her perpetual tipsiness meant that she changed her mind from one day to the next about whether her baseboards should be pink, orange, or lemon-yellow, and required a lot of overtime by his paint crew. Meanwhile, Joe was staying three days a week on Adelia's dime at the Palms Inn, a swanky Magnolia Beach hotel, and eating (and drinking) most of his meals at Tiki Joe's, a retro-cool lounge in town. It sounded fun, honestly, to spend half of December in balmy Florida, but Joe was too depressed about his status with Sophie to enjoy the seventy-five-degree sunshine.

"Plus, Adelia keeps inviting me to luncheons with all her friends," Joe told us gloomily. "Usually I love eating chicken salad with ladies in caftans, but this holiday season, I don't have it in me to booze and schmooze."

He nibbled dispiritedly at a Thai wing, then threw it aside. "I never thought I'd say this, but I actually miss spending hours on end sitting on the man-bench at the Versace boutique, waiting for Sophie to make up her mind between slingbacks or strappy sandals. I must be close to hitting bottom."

Other customers wanted their beer and wings, so for the next fifteen minutes, I had to miss out on the rest of Joe's complaints about Adelia. He was just finishing up regaling Holly with the Eula-suitcase incident when Sophie and Gerda walked through the slightly battered front door of the Pub.

"We have returned, because I have been thinking more about Eula's missing items. If we are to find the loot, we need to follow Eula around and gather clues," Gerda announced. As always, she sounded like a *Game of Thrones* character whose syntax had been influenced by Yoda.

"I agree," said Joe, which surprised me, since he and Gerda rarely see eye to eye. "I want that nine grand from Eula's gold bricks. And Gerda, you've got upper body strength I'm never going to attain, and which we're gonna need to hoist that Samsonite when we find it."

"That's for sure!" said Sophie, violating her no-insults agreement with Joe. "You could barely lift my clutch bag when I asked you to hold it at parties. When we were dating, that is."

"I hate to say it, but we need to put together our own Ocean's 11 to find Eula's missing gold, with Gerda as the muscle of the operation,"." Joe shrugged, while Gerda nodded somewhat smugly.

"Help me get this straight: You're going to spend the holidays trying to find a suitcase belonging to an evil girl who exclusively wears beige swoopy dresses?" said Holly, looking as stressed as I've ever seen her.

"Eula's expanded to a more stylish wardrobe," Joe told Holly. "It's still all beige, though," he admitted.

"Just be careful," said Holly coolly, crossing her skinny jean-clad legs. "Eula's got all that cash now and might invite you to be the Leo DiCaprio to her Kate Winslet on this pricey boat trip."

"I hate Eula, and I'm still going to do everything in my power to make her feel the Grand Canyon–like breadth of my hatred! I'm going to be pissy, petulant, and incredibly persistent in dogging her!" Joe exploded. "After I find the gold bricks, that is."

"Figures," said Sophie, sipping the Sprite I'd handed her, since she's not much of a drinker.

"I don't picture me and Eula at the prow of her cruise ship anytime soon, but if you think I'm going to pass up a chance to get forty thousand dollars of Eula's money, split it four ways, and possibly turn her over to customs, you don't know Joe Delafield!" said Joe, employing the third person.

"Well, here's your chance, because the horrible Eula has just arrived," Gerda told him.

EULA HAD INDEED entered the Pub. She marched over, reached into her shiny beige handbag (probably bought at duty-free), and emerged with an iPad. "I just came by to show you the exact type of suitcase that's missing," she said, bringing up the Samsonite Web site. "It's this one, the thirty-inch Black Label Firelite spinner in deep blue."

"Where's your new boyfriend?" asked Bootsie pointedly.

"He's meeting business associates for a drink," Eula said primly, "and then we're having a late dinner over at Gianni's."

"Does this guy really exist, Eula?" asked Joe.

"Of course he exists!" Eula screamed, losing it and looking a little less like the fancy new version of herself and more like the annoying teenager we'd all known and hated in high school. "He's amazing! He's tan, tall, and wears crisp blue blazers and fantastic striped shirts and has handmade loafers! And he's a lawyer!"

"Uh-huh," said Joe. "And he's staying at your house? Are you guys having lots of steamy lovin' over on Rosebud Lane?"

"He's staying at the home of a *friend*," Eula informed Joe angrily. "And by the way, he's a complete gentleman and we're taking things slow. Also, I'm not going to tell you where he's bunking this week, because I don't want you showing up there and bothering him. You and Bootsie are basically one step removed from stalkers."

Gerda and I looked at Joe and Bootsie for a comeback, which neither of them had, since Eula's assessment was correct.

"Fair enough," acknowledged Joe. "We've stalked a few people in the past. But I still question the existence of your admirer."

"See for yourself," Eula told him, recovering some of her air of calm superiority. "We've got an eight-thirty reservation at Ristorante Gianni. Just so you know where to find me, I'll be at Table 11—the best table in the place—wearing a new Gucci shearling jacket, and I'll be ordering the arugula salad and the lobster pasta for two. See ya!"

WING NIGHT GETS an early crowd, so after cleaning the tables and a quick mop of the floor, I finished my shift at 9:15 p.m. Unfortunately, I looked awful and smelled worse, unless you like the scent of stale wings and fries.

Sophie and Gerda had stayed to drive me to go watch Eula on her dinner date, and to prevent me from sneaking home and going to bed after my long day. I wasn't all that happy about this, but I'd been told it was nonnegotiable: We were all going to check out Eula's new guy.

Joe and Holly were already on-site at Gianni's, having left the Pub at 8:45 to ensure they wouldn't miss a single second of Eula's date. Bootsie, somewhat distracted by sending text after unanswered text to Chip and still feeling the effects of the Xanax she borrowed from Joe, had gone with them.

"I need to go home and take a shower," I told Sophie and Gerda, who were waiting outside for me in Sophie's huge car.

"Ya could use one," agreed Sophie, giving me a dubious sniff. "You look worse than I've ever seen ya, too, but we don't have time to stop at your place if we're gonna see Eula in action on her date. I feel real bad for you, though. I figured you'd be a mess, so I brought you my Cavalli poncho, which is real long and swingy, and I'm gonna do my three-minute makeover on you right here in the car."

"Okay," I said, admitting to myself that deep down, I did want to see Eula's new boyfriend. My car was parked behind The Striped Awning, but I could walk the half mile to the shop in the morning. Waffles and I could use the exercise, actually.

"I need to get home soon, though, to let Waffles out. If he misses his nine-thirty snack, he gets really hungry!" I felt a pang of guilt about leaving Waffles for the whole night. He'd probably slept through the HGTV shows I'd left on to keep him company, but what if his tummy was growling?

"That dog needs strict organic diet of steamed poultry and a few vegetables such as carrots, and should not receive snacks," Gerda informed me. "He looks like he been stuffing his face with Big Macs. Typical American, full of cheese, sauce, and meat."

These words hurt, because occasionally Waffles and I do hit the McDonald's drive-through, but we never get a Big Mac. We share a cheeseburger, hold the onions, which is barely three hundred calories, and Waffles is built along the lines of Kevin James: It would be weird if he was suddenly as gorgeously muscled as, say, a dog version of Alexander Skarsgård. Not everyone's going to be super-fit!

While I fumed silently, Sophie parked in the Gianni driveway, turned around to face me in the backseat of her car, and turned into a one-person glam squad. She spritzed me with a cloud of Versace perfume, threw a cool, fringy black poncho over my head, and aimed some hairspray at my head while whipping the largest round hairbrush I've ever seen through my long brown hair. Within seconds, blush, mascara, and lip gloss somehow flew from Sophie's makeup bag onto my face.

Meanwhile, I noticed that Sophie herself had on an outfit that might have been designed for Britney Spears's Vegas backup dancers. Her dress was roughly the size of a hand towel, super glittery, and strapless, which was surprising considering the temperature had fallen to thirty-five degrees.

Sophie eyed me critically, then took off the pair of swingy drop earrings she was wearing and stuck them into my earlobes. I fingered the baubles, alarmed, since they featured enormous stones that I'd be terrified to wear if they were real.

"Ta-da!" she sang out to me as I took a quick look in her compact mirror, and thanked her. "I took you from chicken wing to awesome bling in a matter of seconds. And don't look so nervous, 'cause those earrings are Diamonique! Six-carat total weight, but only forty-two bucks on QVC!

"Now, let's hustle, girls, because not only do we all want to get an eyeful of this guy of Eula's, but I need to flirt with Channing to make Joe jealous, and also, I'm freezing. A girl can't cover up a dress like this with a parka."

FIFTEEN SECONDS LATER, we were inside Restaurant Gianni, where our eyes immediately zoomed over to Table 11. This table, midway between the bar area and just at the front of the dining room, is considered by people who know (namely, Holly and Sophie) to be the most desirable placement to sit and consume the handmade pastas and wood-fired meat at Gianni's. It offers little in the way of privacy, but does provide a view of every angle of the old firehouse-turned-eatery.

There was Eula, giggling over the lobster while a guy with his back to us leaned over to feed her a twirled-up forkful of spaghetti. His hair was perfectly combed back with a teeny bald spot, his hands were tanned to a Bermuda Gold, and his shirt cuffs were striped and spiffy. He leaned in to give Eula a little squeeze as she chewed and swallowed.

"This is all way too familiar," said Holly. "The starched shirt under the navy blazer. The groping hands. The leaning over and cheesily fawning over Eula . . ."

"Eula's new guy is Scooter Simmons!" shrieked Sophie. "That shady lawyer from Florida!"

Chapter Six

"I SEE YOU'VE eyeballed Eula's new guy," said Joe, when we all managed to collect ourselves and stagger over to where he was seated at the bar with Holly, who was sipping a Pellegrino, and Bootsie, who, like Joe, had a large glass of Scotch in front of her. "I was so shocked that I couldn't even text you. It was all I could do to lift this drink to my lips and gulp."

"Yeah, our old friend Scooter is in town visiting Eula," agreed Channing, emerging from the kitchen to say hi. "I have to say I'm surprised to see him. Scooter just doesn't look right outside his natural habitat, which is on a golf course in Florida."

"I need a cigarette," said Channing's girlfriend Jessica, who as usual looked beautiful and bored. She drifted past us in leather pants, impossibly high heels, and some kind of drapey blouse, headed for a smoke break on the chilly back patio. Jessica doesn't wear things like coats, boots, scarves, or cozy L.L. Bean wool socks, and she doesn't seem to get cold. Maybe all the cigarette smoke has a warming effect, or, as Joe has theorized, she might be part vampire.

It *was* unnerving to see Eula's new man, Scooter Simmons, outside of his usual upscale environs in his native Florida. We'd all met Simmons not quite a year before at a local lounge called Tiki Joe's in swanky Magnolia Beach, Florida.

During our trip, it had been revealed that Scooter and Sophie's estranged husband, Barclay, were secretly plotting to condo-ize a pristine patch of beachfront, and we'd helped prevent the sneaky deal. Scooter had been a frequent customer at a restaurant Gianni had opened down in Florida, and had been involved in any number of illegal deals.

When last we'd seen him, Scooter was being grounded by his stepmother Susie and put on a strict allowance, which was embarrassing since he's in his midforties. I guess Susie had loosened up the purse strings considerably, though, if he could afford even a week on board Eula's ship. Or maybe Scooter had found a new and lucrative business deal which yielded the kind of cash needed for a ticket onto the *Palace of the Seas.*

"I'm trying to imagine what kind of racketeering business Scooter has dreamed up since last we saw him," mused Joe. "The deeds to nonexistent diamond mines and worthless shares in caves filled with secret deposits of platinum are two that spring to mind."

"Channing, we'll take Table 12, please," Holly told the handsome chef. "We'd like to be Eula-adjacent."

"EULA MUST HAVE gone home to change before dinner! She's wearing the sold-out Gucci cropped jacket," whispered Sophie, clearly outraged. "Which I was going to buy myself for Christmas, but all the salesgirls said it had been sent to, like, European movie stars!"

"Hi, Eula," Joe said, as he pulled out our chairs in his usual polite way. "Cute jacket. A word of advice, though, a girl your size shouldn't try to pull off Italian designers, at least in the outerwear category. That coat is wearing you."

"I think you all know my boyfriend, the very handsome and wonderful Scooter!" said Eula, after giving Joe an angry glare.

"Hey, there!" said Scooter, getting up to aim kisses at Holly and Sophie. Naturally, he didn't remember who I was, which was fine with me, even though I'd once had dinner with him, dressed up with hair extensions and huge eyelashes as part of our effort to uncover Scooter's secret condo plans.

Scooter had harbored a serious crush on Holly, and his slightly bloodshot blue eyes lit up when he saw her. Eula, though, was aiming a suspicious eye at him, and Scooter quickly scooted back to his seat next to Eula and began kissing her hand.

I could see that Eula was utterly smitten with her new man, though, and understandably: Scooter is a handsome fellow with extremely good manners. He's honestly quite likable, exuding a golfy bonhomie. He's fun to have drinks with, very well-groomed, and smells fantastic, and will open your car door and pull out your chair attentively while paying you lavish and unlikely compliments (if perhaps finding a way to get someone else to pay the bill). Not everyone has these skills, and frankly, he's a very charming guy. If he hadn't once tried to steal from his own half brother, he might have been the perfect guy for Eula. They could float around the world sipping champagne and golfing their days away, and a permanent cruise is probably the perfect place for Scooter.

"Soooo, you two are in love," said Bootsie. "And you met on a boat," she said, dragging her chair and her wineglass over to Eula and Scooter's table, which Eula didn't look all that happy about. "Can you describe to me the exact moment you fell for Eula?"

"It was on the dance floor!" Scooter said, sipping what looked like . . . a wine spritzer? This was weird, because Scooter in the past had always been gulping down 100-proof martinis and tequila drinks the way other people slurp Gatorade. "Just picture this: a moonlit night, the second one onboard the *Palace of the Seas*, and there's a dinner dance up on the Aloha Deck. We're just floating past Turks and Caicos when, suddenly, this petite vision in a beige gown caught my eye."

"I was wearing Calvin Klein!" Eula piped up. "And Scooter here had on a Ralph Lauren navy blazer, which perfectly matches his gorgeous blue eyes."

"A beige dress and a navy blazer—will wonders never cease," said Joe wearily.

"So we were slow dancing to big-band music, and then the band—the *Palace of the Seas* has its own orchestra, and there are three formal nights a week, outdoors if weather permits—suddenly started playing disco music, and we boogied to Donna Summer, Kool & the Gang, and the Bee Gees. It was during 'Hot Stuff' that Eula and I first kissed," Scooter told us.

"The next day, we went to breakfast together," Eula said. "And we shared Brie omelets, and then went to Zumba, and then did some al fresco painting on Grand Turk island, which was amazing. And that was it!"

"I'm going to get better at tennis to try to keep up with this minx!" Scooter said, prompting a groan from Joe. "And she's going to perfect her golf game, since that's my passion in life. Other than her, of course," he added hastily.

"That's great, but what about your real estate career and your life in Magnolia Beach, Scooter?" demanded Bootsie. "Plus, I thought your stepmom put you on, like, house arrest. How can you afford the hefty ticket to the *Palace of the Seas*, anyway?"

"And did ya quit drinking, Scooter?" asked Sophie. "Last winter, you were one thirsty guy. But I commend you if you gave up martinis. I think maybe it was the wrong drink for you. You might be allergic to vodka, 'cause you got super-drunk real fast every time I saw ya in Florida."

"I've found my freedom and my purpose in life on the high seas," Scooter announced. "With Eula by my side, I have a fresh start. And obviously, I've accumulated a certain amount of savings, and the staggeringly steep price tag to ascend the gangway of the *Palace of the Seas* doesn't represent a financial hardship for me."

He'd begun to perspire a little, though, and Gerda didn't help matters when she held up her phone, upon which she'd been Googling fees for the *Palace of the Seas* and said, "I find this difficult to swallow. Mr., um, Scooter, you would need to be a far more careful person with your finances to afford a trip like this. For instance, this Eula girl bought the two-year ticket to this boat. It says here that the price to ride around on the cruise ship is, like, forty grand a month. Probably whole boat is filled with Powerball winners."

"Of course, the average American can't experience this kind of voyage with stops in Africa, Italy, and Fort Lauderdale!" agreed Scooter. "But I've been very fortunate with my investments, and I happen to have some new investors in my business operations. Excuse me," he added, glancing at his phone and rising from the table. "That's one of my partners calling now, so I'll just step outside and take this.

"Don't move a muscle, you precious little piece of heaven," he told Eula, who gave a modest giggle.

"Gross," observed Gerda.

AFTER FIVE MINUTES, Scooter returned to his table, and the two were served Gianni's famous lobster pasta, while Joe angrily ordered pizzas, salads, and Bolognese pasta for our group. Bootsie added her favorite pappardelle with wild mushrooms, and Holly got her usual: a few spinach leaves topped with a couple of baby carrots.

Despite the fact that I was wearing Sophie's cute poncho and had benefited from her expert backseat makeup application, I still felt like I had been basted in wing sauce. Plus, I'd seen enough of Eula and her new guy. Also, the restaurant brought back painful memories of my first date with John, since we'd had dinner on the patio when Gianni had first opened eighteen months ago. Finally, I begged Bootsie to drive me home.

"We're going to follow Scooter home when he drops off Eula!" Bootsie reminded me. "This isn't about you, Kristin. Or, more accurately, this is about you—and your possible share in the reward of a missing gold brick."

"Ugh, I'm ready to go," moaned Joe, waving his hand despondently in the direction of Eula and Scooter, who were sharing a passion fruit sorbet. "I can't decide which possibility is more depressing: that Eula and Scooter really are in love, or that Scooter's the suitcase-stealing phony that I'm ninety-nine-point-seven percent sure he is. Plus, I just noticed Eula has on a diamond bracelet that looks like she might have gone on a jewelry-buying spree while floating from island to island."

We all looked, not very subtly, at the glimmering ornament on

Eula's wrist. I don't know the first thing about fine jewelry, so it could have been Diamonique, but judging by the reaction Holly and Joe had to the glittery item, it had to be real.

"Maybe it was a gift from Scooter," I suggested, prompting groans and more irate looks.

"Eula's buying her own bling," Sophie informed me. "I know men, and Scooter ain't the type to pull out his credit card in a jewelry shop—just like someone else I know," she said, pointing at Joe.

"Do you think it's possible that Eula is getting her Versace and Gucci sent right from Milan?" asked Holly, looking agitated as she sipped some water. "Is it, like, being sent to Eula care of exotic ports and then loaded onto the *Palace of the Seas*?"

"I was wondering the same thing!" shrieked Sophie. "How is she getting these items we don't know about? Because you know Holly and I don't skimp when it comes to spending on stuff designed by the amazing craftspeople of Italy. Eula must be on some special list!"

Within moments, Scooter had thrown down some cash on his table, Holly signed our bill, and we followed Eula and Scooter Simmons out to the parking lot, where the tanned lawyer made a showy big deal of helping Eula into the passenger seat of a sleek BMW sedan with rental plates Seconds later, as we all headed to our cars, the pair whooshed off into the crisp December night.

That's when we noticed that Jared had moved the Gianni catering truck to a perpendicular angle in front of both Sophie and Holly's cars.

"Jared!" screamed Bootsie. "What the fuck? You parked us in. We need to follow that guy!"

The teenager sheepishly emerged from the front doors of the restaurant and headed toward the white truck with the fancy green Gianni logo, keys at the ready, but by this time, Eula and her new boyfriend were long gone.

"Sorry," said Jared. "That tan guy gave me a hundred dollars to park you guys in while he stepped out here to take a phone call. I feel real bad, but what with the holidays, I need the money."

Bootsie advanced on the hapless kid, who looked terrified, until Holly intervened.

"Jared," she said patiently, "we have a few issues to settle. First of all, weren't you just over at the town square helping Walt?"

"Yeah, I was on duty with Walt till 8, and now I'm on the clock here at Gianni's from 8:30 till 11," Jared told her. "Then I get on Uber from 11 p.m. till 1 a.m., even though I've never actually had anyone request a ride that late. You know this town goes to bed early."

"Whatever," Holly told him. "Now listen up. One, anything Eula and her creepy new friend do, we need to know about. From now on in, I want you to call me or Bootsie, day or night, and I'll pay you for this important information." Cash emerged from Holly's tiny handbag, and Jared nodded happily as he pocketed it. "Secondly, anything they try to bribe you to do, ignore it, and I'll double the going rate."

"Sure!" said Jared. "I'm really sorry!"

"And third, I'm opening Uber accounts for all of us, because Gerda here still doesn't have a license, and we're all planning to drink a lot during the holidays, so we'll need you to drive us around," Holly continued. "Now, what did you hear Scooter—Eula's date—say on that phone call?"

"He said, 'Pete, the package is heading your way,'" Jared reported. "Which I thought was weird, because if it's a FedEx, he could have just texted a tracking number."

"He's probably talking about the Samsonite—or maybe the package is my brother Chip!" said Bootsie, as upset as I've ever seen her. "And we don't know anyone named Pete! Is Chip, like, laid out on ice and being cold-shipped somewhere?"

She texted Chip for about the fortieth time.

"You just saw Chip a few hours ago, and he said he'd be back by Monday. Even if he wasdead in a ditch somewhere right now, or being shipped to an undisclosed location where punishment awaits him, he would not be ice-cold yet," Gerda pointed out logically.

"Gerda, you're too much!" said Sophie hastily, making the "zip it" signal to the Pilates pro and giving Bootsie an encouraging arm pat. "Your brother's probably home and fast asleep in his twin bed up in your mom's attic. Like Chip himself said, don't worry!"

We all headed home, definitely worried. Chip had gone silent.

Chapter Seven

THE NEXT MORNING, we met at the luncheonette to get Joe's *Ocean's 11*-style plan formulated for finding Eula's gold bricks—and hopefully to figure out how to help Chip and find out who shot Sophie's purse.

As I hung up my Old Navy parka on a nearby hook, I noticed that everyone looked a bit worse for wear after sitting in on Eula and Scooter's date night. We all had dark circles under our eyes, and while Joe was his usual flawlessly unwrinkled self, wearing a natty tweed blazer and scarf in lieu of outerwear, and Holly had on one of her flowing sweaters that wrap around her about twenty times, the mood was flustered.

I'd resolved to spend fifteen minutes, tops, in the luncheonette, knowing from past experience that once Joe starts hatching plans, it can take up weeks of time that I should be spending on selling antiques. Plus, I'd arrived home from Gianni's last night hours past my usual bedtime, and had been welcomed with a pair of soulful sad eyes from Waffles, who doesn't like to watch HGTV all by himself. I'd just dropped him off at The Striped Awning with a rawhide chew, but that wouldn't make up for Waffles's injured feelings.

Truthfully, though, I was quite worried about Chip, and hoping Joe or Bootsie would propose a reasonable plan for figuring out what, exactly, was going on with the amiable golf-equipment mogul. Calling the police to report the threatening note seemed like a good idea, but Chip himself *had* asked Bootsie to let him resolve things on his own.

And maybe the incident wasn't such a big deal! Maybe, say, Chip had ordered a bunch of inventory for his golf store for the holidays, and been unable to pay his suppliers to the tune of fifty grand?

"In my opinion, all of yesterday's misdemeanors, especially the missing gold bricks, are somehow linked to Scooter," said Bootsie, sucking down some cranberry juice.

"Ya think Scooter shot my purse? The Santa guy looked younger and skinnier. My Santa wasn't Scooter," Sophie told her.

"Sure, but once we get the goods on Scooter and the gold, I have a feeling the whole Christmas crime wave is going to unravel," Bootsie told her. "Who knows? Maybe Scooter's involved in the moonshine heist, too, although it's hard to picture Scooter fitting an entire five-gallon still complete with a wort mixer and heating device in a rented BMW. And by the way, can we order some food, please? I'm having the huevos rancheros and a side of Gruyère grits."

While Bootsie asked our waiter for this cheesy breakfast, I reflected on how much the little eatery has expanded its breakfast offerings since the Bryn Mawr Country Club's chef revamped the menu last summer. While the place looks the same, with reassuring linoleum floors, a long counter, and Formica booths, you can now get short-rib hash, a cheddar waffle with Amish-style bacon, and asparagus and chèvre quiche.

The rest of us chose more modest dishes: Gerda got egg whites and a kale smoothie. Holly got a thimble-size ramekin of berries, and Sophie ordered a donut, while Joe and I went for classic scrambled eggs. We all stared as Holly pushed aside the fruit, then asked for a side of white toast with butter, and actually ate it.

"You know there is gluten in that, right?" Gerda asked Holly. "I thought you did not consume this harmful wheat product."

"I can't seem to eat anything except toast and crackers lately," said Holly. "I've been a little nauseous."

"Maybe you are expecting a baby," Gerda informed her.

We all stared at Gerda, shocked by her wild conjecture, and then at Holly's midsection. Her belly was partly blocked by the Formica diner table and swathed in layers of fancy sweater, but appeared to be as flat as ever. For her part, Holly froze in place, half a piece of toast falling to her plate.

I thought to myself that this would be great news! Holly was a loyal and devoted person who'd make a fantastic mom, and Howard would no doubt love to be a dad. It just seemed unlikely for some reason—I mean, Bootsie had always wanted kids, and had immediately produced two within a few years of getting married in her midtwenties. But Holly had helmed so many town events lately and Howard traveled so much for work that bringingforth human life hadn't been mentioned, at least to the rest of us.

"When was the last time ya, you know, got some lovin' with Howard?" Bootsie asked.

"Maybe your hubby knocked ya up at Thanksgiving," offered Sophie, adding, "Why don't you just take one of those drugstore tests? This could be real cute for the holidays!"

"I'm too busy to be pregnant right now," Holly told her. "And I'm not going to have time before the twenty-fifth to pee on a stick. Let's get back to the *Ocean's 11* plans."

"That movie is based on the same idea as Robin Hood," Bootsie said. "Steal from the rich. Or in this case, steal from Scooter, the guy who *already* stole from the rich."

"I thought Andy Garcia was the hottest guy in *Ocean's 11*!" announced Sophie. "He's so handsome."

"But all the people in the movie had special talents, like safe-cracking and dealing cards and temporarily disabling giant casino security systems," I said. "We don't have, well, any useful skills."

"Gerda hacks computers, and I'm great at picking locks with a safety pin, as long as they're not too secure and were made before, say, 1978, which most locks in this town were," Bootsie informed me. "What else could we possibly need?"

"Can someone track down all the black SUVs with Jersey plates that start with an S? That's a big clue from the purse shooting and outside the Pub with Chip. And if I get the list of Jersey SUV owners, I might know the owner as one of Barclay's old cronies, and Gerda could go rough the guy up and we'd also probably find your brother," Sophie told Bootsie. "I hate to say it, but it sounds like Chip fucked up and got himself knee-deep in the linguini, if ya know what I mean."

"What does this mean? He ate too much pasta?" asked Gerda.

"She means he messed with the wrong guys. And Sophie, there are probably like two hundred thousand SUVs in Jersey with license plates starting with S," Bootsie told her.

"Yeah, but how many of them are being around driven by Santa with a gun?" Sophie replied, almost making a logical point.

"Let me see that note again," Sophie added to Bootsie, who

handed over the missive Chip had received the night before. "When Barclay would try to scare people, there was usually another message hidden inside threatening notes. See how this piece of paper is double-folded? It's a little mobster trick."

She unfolded the paper, and read, "To Chip's family: Don't contact the police or we'll chop off Chip's eyelashes, including most of the eyelid, and send it to you baked into a flatbread pizza. Merry Christmas."

We all stopped eating, and Bootsie looked pale. "That's it," she announced. "If I don't hear from Chip by tomorrow, I'm calling the police."

"Do you think Chip got in over his head with some golf-equipment suppliers and couldn't pay up when they delivered the putters and drivers?" I asked hopefully. Honestly, even to myself, this theory didn't sound all that likely.

"It sounds more like he borrowed money from someone who isn't too flexible with their payment plan!" Sophie told me.

"Isn't that Mrs. Potts getting out of her station wagon?" interrupted Joe. "Looks like she's got her arm in a sling."

Honey Potts, the town's sixtysomething doyenne and owner of its largest and most venerated estate, parked her car and emerged with one arm trussed up in a large silk scarf-turned-sling, and a glass of what appeared to be vodka in the other. Limping slightly, she made her way across the short expanse near the town's pergola and came into the luncheonette.

"Mrs. P., I didn't know ya were injured!" said Sophie. "What happened?"

"Ironically, it's holiday-related," Mrs. Potts told us. "I was on my stepladder and arranging garlands on top of my grandmother's Georgian mirror over the fireplace, and the ladder malfunctioned. Whole thing collapsed," she said, adding that she'd landed next to the liquor cabinet.

Luckily, she explained, she hadn't hit her head as she'd fallen from her perch above an eight-foot-high mantel, but had landed on her shoulder. Her nephew Mike Woodford, who lives in a cottage on her estate and runs the place for her, had been due to help her hang further greenery above the massive front doors of Sanderson, so she'd merely sipped a drink and waited till he arrived. At that point, Mike (full disclosure: I've shared several steamy kissing sessions in the past with this guy) had taken her to the ER, where she'd been diagnosed with a bad sprain.

"Anyhow, I won't be able to run the town holiday festival this year," she added, looking as disappointed as she ever does—which isn't all that devastated. Pottses don't believe in showing emotion. Also, maybe the grande dame felt a sense of relief at skipping the festival gig, which looks like a ton of work. There are square dancers, elves, the singers, a photo area, and food trucks to organize, and it's usually freezing.

"I feel so bad for ya!" said Sophie. "I hate to think of ya splat on the floor, facedown by the booze. Hey, guess what!" Sophie added. "Since Joe and I split up, and my heart was shattered, stomped on, and smothered by him, *I'll* do the holiday festival this year!

"I'm thinking, um, a Martinis and Mistletoe theme. Or a Winter Wonderland with Hot Whiskey. Or Christmas in the Islands, with blender drinks!"

"Okay," said Mrs. Potts, who seemed to approve of the all-alcohol-related inspirations Sophie was dreaming up. "Consider yourself in charge. Also, I'm supposed to start decorating the whole town tomorrow, which I do every December."

"I could help Sophie do this for you," announced Gerda, as we all swiveled toward her in amazement.

"Huh," mused Mrs. Potts. "Don't you work for this one here's ex-husband, forcing him to exercise and eat right?" She poked her fork toward Sophie.

"I run a Pilates studio, work part-time at the fancy wine shop owned by Holly, and sometimes help out Mr. Shields, but he's at a health spa in Nevada right now," Gerda told her. "Thanksgiving was not a good week for him and he's on doctor's orders to hike for at least three hours daily. Anyway, if you would like to come take a Pilates class with me when your sprain is healed, it's free for you. I have respect for your hard work ethic and quiet strength. You have a European way of dealing with the problems in life. You don't complain."

"Okay." Honey Potts shrugged. "Um, thanks. And you and Sophie have the town festival job. The decorating committee meets at 10 a.m. tomorrow. The whole committee is basically just the Colketts, so you can work out the details with them—who, by the way, just walked in," she added, as the handsome designers waved from the front counter, where they were picking up a takeout order.

"Maybe I take one corner of town square to feature the European holiday legend of Krampus," mused Gerda. "That could be very educational for the children."

"What, that horror movie?" said Bootsie. "That's some scary shit, Gerda."

"They exaggerate in that film," Gerda told her defensively. "In Bavaria, Krampus is fun Yuletide fable, gives kiddies a thrill."

"I saw that movie on cable one night, and I haven't slept eight hours straight since," Joe announced. "It's an evil half man, half goat who steals kids."

"Let's not do the Krampus corner," said Mrs. Potts. "Creative idea, though," she told Gerda.

"Hey, Chan!" called out Sophie, as the movie-star-ish chef joined the crowd in the diner. "And Tim and Tom, over here! We're planning the town festival with ya. Mrs. Potts here took a tumble and is out of commission for a coupla weeks."

"Sorry to hear that, Mrs. P.," Tom Colkett told the doyenne. "I hope you've got a ton of good pain meds."

"By the way, Sophie, we can help you out with your new career as cabaret chanteuse!" piped up Tim Colkett enthusiastically, while Tom shot him a look that shouted, *No!*

It was too late for Tom to quash the idea of joining in on Sophie's performance. Tim was already miming playing keyboards. "I'm a talented jazz pianist, and Tom here is excellent on the stand-up bass. We're practically ready for Radio City, honestly, but we had to choose between our music and our design and landscaping skills, and we went with design as our main gig."

"I didn't know that!" said Sophie, jumping out of the booth to give both guys big hugs. "This is going to be awesome!"

"Honestly, doll, we're a little scared to spend time with you, though, after that shooting incident yesterday," Tom informed Sophie. "What if you had been carrying, say, one of those tiny Dolce & Gabbana lace pouchettes? That wouldn't have stopped a .38-caliber bullet."

"Don't worry about it!" Sophie told him. "That kind of little drive-by is nothing in Jersey. Barclay's probably bored out in Nevada, and trying to get one more zinger in before I sign the divorce papers. Plus, that Santa has moved on! He's now after this one's brother," she said, indicating Bootsie.

"Colketts, you're the backup musicians," agreed Channing. "Plus, you can decorate the restaurant for Christmas. Unfortunately, Gianni gave me a limited budget: three thousand bucks."

This sounded like a lot to me, but the Colketts started talking about hot glue guns, and what a cheapo Chef Gianni was, and how they were hoping against hope he'd decide to stay in Beverly Hills and ruin everyone on that coast's Christmas, when Bootsie interrupted.

"We need to get back to helping Chip," she announced. "And, and this is much lower down on the list, to Scooter and Eula." The Colketts, Channing, and Mrs. Potts headed to seats at the counter, while we got down to business.

"This should be easy," said Bootsie. "We start tonight by following Eula."

"I hope that girl Eula isn't gonna get, like, thrown off a bridge somewhere," said Sophie. "She's real annoying, but I'd hate to see her dead over a bagful of gold bars."

"People like Eula don't die till they're about one hundred and five," Bootsie told her. "You can't get rid of her. I mean, look at her. She's on a round-the-world cruise, and she's still back here bothering us. Chip, on the other hand, I'm worried about."

"Your brother got problems," agreed Gerda. "I suggest you head to his golf shop and ransack the place for clues. Like, right now."

Chapter Eight

Chip's store was really nice, I thought, as Bootsie unlocked the doors and turned on the lights. I'd picked up Waffles at The Striped Awning and met her at Golf Sweet Golf, which I'd never visited before. It was located several blocks from my shop on a charming corner close to Restaurant Gianni, and had a clubby, man-cave-ish decor, with two large-screen TVs, a small complimentary bar with a decanter of Scotch, and a mini-refrigerator full of beer. There was a wall of seasonal golf sweaters, polos, and embroidered corduroy pants for golfers who play all year round.

There were a half-dozen stations for various types of clubs and golf bags, gloves and visors, golf balls and golf books. All told, though, the store wasn't all that much bigger than The Striped Awning, maybe one thousand square feet. How exactly had Chip earned enough for that pricey new truck?

"Chip's involved in a phony golf resort," Bootsie announced after five minutes of rifling through her brother's papers. "Look at this prospectus!"

I followed her back to a little seating area where a glossy printed booklet titled *L'Etoile: A Golf Destination* was displayed.

The first page read, "European luxury and international flair have arrived on the tropical shores of South Florida with L'Etoile, a sexy, five-star hotel and residential haven for the discriminating golfer! Alongside an emerald-hued course designed by preeminent golf star Angus MacFayden, L'Etoile will offer the most luxurious dining, spa treatments, pool area with outdoor day club, meditation cabanas, dock space for yachts, and much more!"

In teeny print under this description, "L'Etoile, LLP, is a partnership of PPS Investments and Chip Delaney."

"This place looks really high-end," I said, surprised, as I turned the pages and admired computer-rendered images of an imposing hotel entrance, a glossy white marble lobby area, luxurious restaurants, and beachside cabanas complete with imaginary staff delivering cold drinks on silver trays. A dozen pages were devoted to the golf course and clubhouse, and there were more images of a gorgeous spa, condos, several bars, and a disco. There wasn't a specific address for the hotel, but the prospectus did mention that it was located on glamorous but tranquil Swan Key, Florida.

Toward the end of the book were some pages titled "Special Opportunities for Initial Buyers," which listed whopping prices to own small luxury suites at L'Etoile. One-bedroom units started at five hundred thousand dollars, and there was a hefty monthly club fee (which did include a free facial and massage every four months), and the bigger units were priced from seven hundred thousand dollars and up. L'Etoile hotel rooms were also slated to be very posh with prices to match, and the on-site bistro and steakhouse promised all organic ingredients with handmade pastas, hand-rolled sushi, and hand-picked baby veggies.

"It looks like L'Etoile is offering shares of ownership in the hotel, too, that give you a month or two a year there, as long as you don't mind being in Florida in July and August," I said, scanning the papers, puzzled. "Look, it lists initial investors as the Binghams!" The Binghams are town fixtures usually perched on the porch of the country club sharing a bottle of white zinfandel. They're devoted golfers and gardeners, and a pleasantly boozy couple who'd briefly been kidnapped during the previous summer's tomato show, but had ended up drinking so much during their abduction that they thought they'd actually been on a fun weekend getaway.

"I know the Binghams have a lot of money, but I'm surprised they'd want to get involved in a Florida real estate deal. They don't travel much and this seems kind of glitzy for them."

Bootsie was looking angrier and more confused as she leafed through each page, and her sky-blue eyes were popping as she waved the booklet at me. "Does this look like a deal my brother, who repeated Algebra I at Bryn Mawr Prep, could put together?"

Since I'd also struggled mightily in algebra, I mulled this over for a second, but realized the question was rhetorical.

"Do the concepts of my brother Chip, who wore flip-flops to my wedding, and a hotel called L'Etoile with a marble lobby, a disco, and meditation cabanas make for a likely combination?" Bootsie demanded, heading to the store's bar and pouring herself a midmorning shot of Scotch.

"This hotel and resort really don't seem like a place Chip would dream up," I agreed. "He's more of a beer and burgers guy. Isn't his favorite hotel Crane's in Delray Beach?"

"Of course it is. He was conceived at Crane's, and none of the Delaneys or McElvoys stay at hotels that don't offer kitchenettes or have tiki bars," said Bootsie. She'd shown me Crane's last winter; it was a beautiful, shady oasis in the cool and funky town of Delray, with brightly painted cottages and hotel rooms with a totally charming look. It was the opposite of the glossy plans for L'Etoile, which also looked amazing, in a completely different way.

I looked at the price tag on a Titleist Hybrid in the display next to where we sat, which read two hundred and forty-nine dollars. Maybe the markup on these items *was* such that Chip could have bought that pricey car, I thought to myself. Although this small store, with what had to be a hefty rent given its proximity to the town's best restaurant, couldn't have earned enough for Chip to become a key investor in an upscale resort—could it?

"Hellooo," said a chirpy, upbeat voice a moment later, which turned out to be emanating from Bootsie's and Chip's mom, Kitty Delaney, who bustled in wearing a cheery, bright red Lands' End jacket. "I got your message. What's this about Chip?" she asked Bootsie, who was back behind the counter, upending Chip's trash can. "Oh, and Kristin and your doggie, how cute," she added, patting Waffles on his head as he wagged up at her.

"Your son—my brother, the golf and tennis club champion who you once told me you and Dad conceived after one too many margaritas in Delray Beach, Florida—is on the lam!" Bootsie informed her mom.

Kitty, who's an adorable, gossipy, and preppy woman who wears coral lipstick and likes to imbibe Bloody Marys and garden, looked dubious, then broke into a laugh. "Chip left me a message that he's going to be out of town for a few days. He's fine."

"Mummy, Chip is not fine," Bootsie told her. "Someone left

him a threatening note saying he owes them fifty thousand dollars, and then Chip suddenly looked really scared, but then told me the same BS story he told you and took off. That's weird!"

"Did Chip put you up to this?" Kitty hooted, plunking herself down on a bench. "You and your brother are terrible! This reminds me of the time Chip told me he needed one hundred and fifty dollars for college textbooks, but actually spent it on hosting a keg party. I'm on to you two and your funny business!"

"This isn't a joke, Mummy!"

"Is Chip hiding out at your house, Bootsie?" hooted Kitty. "Because I'm making lasagna tonight, so you might want to tell him to come home."

"He's missing and probably being held at gunpoint by crazed golf-resort gangsters!" screamed Bootsie.

"Kristin, will you tell her to stop with the jokes," said Kitty, gathering up her handbag and telling Bootsie she had a lot of holiday shopping to do, that Dad wanted gloves for Christmas, and if Bootsie, Will, and the kids wanted to come over tonight, too, Kitty could make an extra lasagna. "Bye, girls." Kitty waved, and headed toward the door.

Bootsie sighed and held up a bunch of envelopes. "Chip hasn't even opened his mail in weeks, and there are no holiday decorations up in the store, and, look—here's a memo in which he told all the employees to take the month off."

"Hello, Mrs. Mother of Bootsie," said Gerda politely, entering the store as Kitty was leaving.

"Did your mother give any clues to the location of your brother?" Gerda added to Bootsie.

"She doesn't even think Chip is missing," Bootsie told her

dispiritedly. "I need you to hack into his laptop, Gerda. It's right here, behind the counter."

"Sure, I do that, no problem," Gerda agreed, cracking her knuckles and looking happy. Gerda loves nothing more than reading people's e-mail and reviewing their bank balances online. I'm not sure exactly how she finds out passwords and usernames, but she's excellent at snooping through personal information.

"If it's okay, I take computer with me, because I am about to head to Le Spa to teach a class. Then, I will dig into Chip's computer," Gerda told Bootsie. "I fast-walk to spa now."

"How are your classes going?" Bootsie said. "Are you still minting money over there, with a waiting list and lines out the door?"

"Bust Your Ass Pilates classes are doing awesome," Gerda told us proudly. "All my group sessions are selling out like crazy. Plus, I still on payroll of Sophie's ex, because when he comes back from Nevada, I need to be ready to start his workouts again. So, basically, I am getting rich."

I sighed, feeling a surge of jealousy. It was true—Gerda's classes were really popular, and Ursula, who owns Le Spa, lets Gerda use a large space in her beauty emporium rent-free. It makes sense, since some of the Pilates clients then stay for a manicure or to get their hair done, and Ursula wasn't using the room, anyway. Still, Gerda lives with Sophie, doesn't own a car, and was still getting paid by Barclay. What was I doing wrong?

"I can give you a ride to Le Spa," I told her, since it was in the forties outside and my store is right across the street from her studio.

"Thank you, no," Gerda told me. "If everyone in this country walked more, there would be far fewer health problems. I come from mountainous area where people live to be, like, one hundred and ten years old due to steep hilly climb to pick up fresh food."

I could tell that Gerda was about to criticize me, Waffles, and our Dunkin' Donuts drive-through habit, so I made a hasty exit.

"GERDA'S HAVING TROUBLE infiltrating Chip's laptop," Bootsie told me when she stopped by my store at 5 p.m. "On the plus side, I opened up the store and sold three clubs, a cardigan sweater, and some golf gloves today. Anyway, Gerda promised to get into Chip's e-mail by breakfast time tomorrow.

"And, since it's Steak Night at the country club, I called over there on a hunch and asked what time Eula's dinner reservation was for tonight. Ronnie said Eula preordered a porterhouse steak for two at 7 p.m. and a special chocolate dessert that's supposedly delicious and only forty calories.

"Anyway, this time Scooter isn't going to get away from us! We're going to hide in that grove of sycamores by the entrance and follow him after dinner to his secret lair."

Chapter Nine

I DON'T GO often to Steak Night, since the giant hunks of meat served at the club are quite pricey.

And speaking of hunks, the first person I saw when we walked in was Mike Woodford, who was sitting in the bar—in the exact seat where I'd first met my boyfriend John a year and a half ago.

"How's John the vet?" asked Mike.

Maybe I should go ahead and tell Mike, on whom I've long had a crush, that my boyfriend John was MIA. I never would have guessed that a veterinarian would be out of town every other month. There were conferences on bovine medicine and on ruminant breeding that lured John to points far-flung all summer, and now, in the middle of winter, he was away on *another* job out of town. Since I wasn't all that happy about it, feeling abandoned and then feeling angry at myself for feeling that way, I hadn't told anyone that he was away, and was hoping none of my friends would notice.

So far, no one except Mike had asked where John was, but I knew this couldn't last. Christmas is prime dating season! If your boyfriend is missing, people take note. Since I had gotten a text from John earlier in which he claimed to miss me, I decided not to share my woes with Mike.

"John's doing great!" I said quickly.

"It seems like he's been out of town a lot this year," Mike observed. "What's going on with you two?"

My heart did two flips and I gulped. *Now* Mike was asking me this? At Christmastime, the most pressure-filled month of the year, when people who are dating for any length of time start to think about commitment—or in my case, start to wonder why their boyfriend is a no-show for the entire month? Plus, Mike's scruffy hot-guy persona has always been just that—he's the hot guy across the street who jokes around with me at the Pub or at occasional parties which he attends with his aunt, Honey Potts.

"I have to go!" I told him. "There's a Eula Morris situation. But, um, I'll get back to you!"

"What's the situation?" Mike asked.

"Eula's missing eight gold bricks worth approximately three hundred twelve thousand dollars," I told him. "Which Eula's new boyfriend might have stolen from her. You've met him," I added to Mike. "She's dating Scooter Simmons from Magnolia Beach, Florida." I briefly outlined the events of the past two days.

"So you're here to get liquored up, and then park Bootsie's car in the bushes and wait for Eula and her date to come out so you can follow them and look for the suitcase?" guessed Mike.

"That's pretty much it," I agreed. "We're hiding in the sycamore grove, though, not bushes."

"I need to hear how this works out," Mike told me, shaking his head. "Maybe we should have dinner this weekend. I'll call you."

This left me puzzled.

Call me? Mike almost never called me. I think he had once dialed my number last summer to tell me that his aunt Honey had a bumper zucchini crop, and he was leaving a bag of squash on my doorstep. That was it. Maybe Mike was finally going to be a serious contender as a boyfriend! And if John wasn't always traveling, this wouldn't matter, but it did!

"Eula's at Table 6! She and Skipper are sharing the beet salad! I hope that crazy bitch eats fast!" Joe said, popping up between me and Mike.

"And there are the Binghams," pointed out Bootsie, eyeing these country-club fixtures at a small table for two, where they were happily working on some steak frites and their favorite pink wine. "I need to ask them about the investment they made in Chip's golf resort. Be right back."

"Yoo-hoo," yelled the Colketts, who were at the large table in the back of the clubby, comfortable bar. "Have a drink with us and we can talk turkey! Or whatever it is we're serving at the holiday party you're planning, Holly. *Is* it gonna be turkey?" All of us except Bootsie squeezed in around the decorators, while Eula aimed a nasty glare our way, then returned to her date with Scooter.

"Seriously, Holly, the town festival is one thing, but this holiday party you're planning for the club staff needs to be better than the Cannes Film Festival's opening night," Tim told her. "And why again is it staff only?"

"Club members can come, but I wanted the staff to have fun this year," Holly told him. "Making food for fifty people at the holidays is stressful for Ronnie, Skipper, Abby, and everyone else who works here. So I told them *I* was hosting them! But then I forgot that no other restaurants in town are open that day to handle the catering, and I couldn't get anyone in Philly to commit to a Christmastime catering job except for one pasta joint down by the stadium. They said they'd do trays of ziti, sausage and meatballs, and to be honest, I got nervous, and nauseous, and I panicked. Then when I called back the next day, the pasta place was all booked up. I also don't have a theme, a waitstaff, or a band."

"Meatballs and sausage is what people *want* to eat," Bootsie told her, returning from the Binghams' table. "That's, like, everyone's favorite meal. You should have booked the meatballs!"

"She's right, hon," Tim Colkett told Holly, who still looked doubtful. "Call the ziti place back and offer to pay double."

"The Trendy Tent is on board, at least, for a heated thirty-by-forty-five-foot pop-up enclosure that will turn my back patio into a party space. And Tim here called me today with a new idea for making the tent look like a Hobbit cave, or something," said Holly vaguely. "What was that again, guys?"

"We were going to build long communal tables entirely out of moss and twigs, and do, like, waterfalls of vodka and food served on tree bark," explained Tim. "The waiters could be dressed up like Orlando Bloom's character in flowing brown robes."

"Not that that isn't an amazing idea, but I don't think anyone will like tree bark or robes, plus we don't have any food," Holly told him. "The vodka waterfall is cool, though."

"How about a vegan party?" suggested Gerda. "That would be fun. People could try new foods, and there would be no alcohol served."

"You're such a kidder!" Tom Colkett told Gerda merrily. "What a hoot."

"I was not joking," Gerda said sourly.

"I'd go back to the vodka fountain," Joe announced.

"How about Lady Gaga as the theme?" Sophie said. "The meat dress alone could inspire a ton of fun stuff!"

"That reminds me, Tim and I were down in Delaware two weeks ago looking for this greenhouse that supposedly grows groves of ten-foot-tall orange trees all winter, when we stumbled onto this roadside stand selling barbecue, which was the best," Tom said.

"I think 'stumbled' is the key word," observed Joe. "Were you guys drinking?"

"We might have had a small one before we left," Tim allowed. "But I don't think we both could have hallucinated a brisket sandwich that was as tender as this one. Plus, there were sweet potato fries, slaw, and some kind of burger you wouldn't believe."

"Are you sure you weren't watching *Diners, Drive-Ins and Dives* and got confused that you actually went there?" asked Bootsie. "That happens to me sometimes when I've had a couple drinks."

"I'm pretty sure we were really there. Anyway, all we need to do is find this place again, hire the BBQ guy to cater your party, and you've got a theme!" Tim told her.

"I'm picturing holiday movies playing on a big screen, a keg, a Bloody Mary bar, a man cave with cigars, and Sophie can do some Elvis Christmas songs!" Tom said. "And, um, spruce branches and a giant tree."

We all stared at the Colketts.

"That sounds like a normal, fun Christmas party," Bootsie finally said, downing some pinot noir "I *love* this idea."

"Howard would probably like that," admitted Holly. "He loves brisket. And fries."

"There's one small problem," said Tim. "We can't remember where the barbecue guy is in Delaware."

"So get another brisket person," Bootsie told them. "Brisket's always good. People love it."

"It has to be this guy!" Tom said, waving down the waiter for another vodka. "Everything depends on his tender, melt-in-your-mouth, marinated, messy masterpiece!"

"The party won't work without that guy," agreed Tim, digging into a filet.

"I research this for you," Gerda told them. "What do you remember about this establishment? Which sounds very unhealthy, by the way."

"It was a wooden shack kind of thing, and the guy served out of a window," Tom said vaguely. "And it had a name that sounded Southern."

"That sounds like every barbecue joint in the whole world!" screamed Bootsie. "Now you've got me into this idea, and you don't know where the guy is?"

"We'll get Jared to Uber you to Delaware this week, you'll find the guy, and we'll have a holiday party that Howard will actually want to attend. This sounds like a plan," said Holly.

"Good, because Eula and Scooter are sawing into that porterhouse steak, which means they'll be finished eating in approximately twenty-eight minutes," said Joe. "Time for us to head for Bootsie's Range Rover and that grove of sycamores. This stakeout is going down for real!"

IT WAS CROWDED in the Range Rover, and there was a lot of arguing about whether the heat was on too high, why it was hot in the front but freezing in the backseat, and how this was boring, and someone should have brought snacks.

Fifteen minutes in, I was still thinking about Mike Woodford.

Maybe he'd changed! The holidays wreaked havoc with most people's emotions, and maybe Mike had suddenly found himself wishing he wasn't single this December, and had decided I was the girl for him!

"Do you think I should go out to dinner with Mike Woodford?" I asked the group while we waited, the SUV concealed by the moonlit patch of trees. "Because he asked me on a date. At least, I think he did. He used the word 'maybe.'"

"Where's your boyfriend?" said Sophie. "You guys have been going out for, like, over a year. In fact, you've been dating that guy as long as me and my ex-Honey Bunny up there in the driver's seat." She glared at Joe, which he probably couldn't see in the dark and from her perch on the backseat.

"Is John the vet as resistant to getting married as certain other men?" added Sophie meaningfully, staring daggers into Joe's back. "Because if he is, I say go out with the hot, scruffy guy Mike!"

"I don't know if John ever wants to get married again," I admitted. "We never talk about it. I'm not sure I want to, either," I amended.

"You should stay with John and get more serious," Holly told me. "You two are perfect together. You both actually like having tons of dogs around and think things like grilling burgers for dinner is fun."

I didn't think these two line items made me and John much different from most of the world, but since Holly isn't into dogs or burgers, she thought this made us unusually compatible.

"You aren't getting any younger," Gerda told me. "This means you should stay away from sexy neighbor. Those guys never work out."

While I felt enraged by Gerda's rude observation—and she

had to be at least the same age as me, if not older—she had a point.

"It's not like Kristin is *that* old," said Joe. "Plus, she has her own business, and she has that house she inherited from her grandparents. So she's independent."

"She does not make much money," Gerda announced. "I mean, she sells old stuff and barely earns enough to buy soup for her dinner. On the other hand, I go into Pilates business just six months ago, and I'm making boatload of cash. This one is not practical." Here, she indicated me.

"Where is John, anyway?" asked Sophie. "'Cause we haven't seen him since, like, before Thanksgiving."

"Did the veterinarian dump you?" asked Gerda. "Because we all figured he broke up with you and you were too embarrassed to tell us. We all been talking about it for last two weeks."

"He's staying rent-free in a cottage on an estate somewhere in California!" I finally yelled defensively. "He's there for three weeks to help take care of two fancy poodles that get massages every day! He's making sure they stay in tiptop shape for the next season of dog shows. Or something like that," I added. "Also, the poodles have a YouTube channel, and they have a ton of subscribers, and they might be getting their own show on Reelz!"

I'd been embarrassed to admit that my boyfriend had temporarily become a "concierge vet" to a couple of fancy dogs, but now the truth was out. The pair of poodles were in training for the Westminster show, and John had been offered such a hefty fee to oversee their canine boot camp that he was spending most of December away from me.

He'd mentioned me flying out for a few days, but I was trying to run a business during the holiday shopping season. Truthfully, though, I realized now that I *should* have gone to visit him. Here I was, sitting in a grove of sycamores waiting to follow a guy named Scooter, when I could have been with my boyfriend in sunny California. Even John's pack of beige dogs of various sizes had gone to California with him.

"And you're here trying to sell antique plates when you could be drinking white wine in California?" Sophie said, squinching up her face in puzzlement. "Didn't John ask ya to visit him?"

"You don't want to leave Waffles, do you?" said Bootsie. Bootsie knew me too well. Waffles was the biggest reason I hadn't gone—the dog and I had never spent a Christmas apart!—along with the fact that I really wasn't sure where my relationship with John was headed.

"I could watch this dog for you and put him on strict diet," Gerda told me.

"No, thanks!" I said hastily, picturing Gerda running a bewildered Waffles on a treadmill.

"I'll take care of your dog," said Holly. "I mean, Martha will do it, she actually loves that mutt," she said, sounding mystified. "You should leave for California ASAP. And, maybe in the meantime, you should go out to dinner with Mike Woodford!"

"Where the hell is Scooter?" asked Joe. "My right leg is asleep, and I can't feel my toes."

"You know what's weird?" said Bootsie. "Scooter wasn't drunk last night."

This was odd, I realized. When we'd seen Simmons in January back in Florida, he'd been completely plastered every night.

"Speaking of which, can one of you please reach into the back of the car, because I happened to hit Liquor World this week," Joe said, "and this feels like a chug-from-the-bottle kind of situation." Bootsie obliged, and handed over the goods.

"You could get arrested for that," said Gerda ominously. "Open container in car is illegal."

"Oh, okay," scoffed Joe, upending a bottle of Maker's Mark into his mouth and gulping down a healthy swig. "Like some policeman's going to be lurking back in the trees, too. Anyway, guys like Scooter can give up booze for a few weeks at a time when there's money at stake," said Joe. "But eventually, dating Eula's going to send him on a tear of epic proportions."

"I'm still wondering about my ex Barclay, speaking of guys who are bonkers," said Sophie. "What was the point of him having someone shoot my purse? Real hit men don't miss, and they don't hit your handbag by mistake. So I'm not scared, but why do that to me? Especially since we're almost divorced and I'm about to start dating a lot of hot, eligible guys! And ones who don't drink in the car!" she added pointedly, as Joe swigged angrily at his bottle.

"Anyway, you want to talk challenging—try getting the Colketts to approve a Swarovski-crystal-encrusted dress for a sultry singing performance!" Sophie announced. "Check these out, girls. I mean, do these little minidresses say Christmas or what? And the Colketts said all of these were 'too sparkly,' which I told them isn't in my dictionary, especially at the holidays!"

Sophie showed us pics of fourteen possible dresses she'd gone to the mall and bought for her performance, asking if we thought three wardrobe changes for a six-song set was too many.

"Enough with the dresses. I never thought we'd see Scooter again," said Joe. "And with Eula Morris, of all people."

"Scooter is married," said Gerda disapprovingly. "Remember,

his wife show up when he was on a date with Holly at Tiki Joe's, and the wife threw Holly's car keys on roof of the store across the street?"

"I always liked his wife after that," Holly reflected. "I didn't have time to explain to her that I was merely pumping her hubby for information. Which maybe wouldn't have made her feel all that much better about him being out at a bar with another woman," she added.

"Does anyone else think it's strange that suddenly Eula wins Powerball, gets on this fancy boat, and within days, her new boyfriend is Scooter?" I asked. I felt bad for Eula, who's certainly attractive enough, but hasn't been all that lucky in love—something I can relate to.

"A scam artist like Scooter probably sets sail a couple times a year," said Bootsie. "What I need to know is if Scooter ever got divorced, or if he's going to break Eula's heart."

"I'll text Adelia Earle's butler Ozzy," offered Joe. "He'll have the scoop on Scooter and Mary Simmons, and whether they're still legally man and wife." Joe tapped at his phone until a pair of approaching headlights gave him pause.

"It's Scooter's BMW! Take this bottle, somebody, I'm driving!"

We followed a quarter mile behind his car, keeping Scooter within sight as he dropped off Eula at her small house on Rosebud Lane. After walking her in and giving her a modest kiss good night, he climbed back into his BMW, then turned left, followed Main Street for a mile, and went down Camellia Lane and turned into the driveway of a house I knew all too well, and never wanted to set foot in again. I froze in terror. To be honest, I make it a point not to go anywhere near Camellia Lane, and try to take alternate routes so as not to pass it.

"Scooter's staying at Mariellen Merriwether's house!" screamed Bootsie. "Do you think he's a golf-playing, blue-blazer-wearing con artist who breaks into unused houses and drinks all the booze?"

"Con artist and booze thief, yes," said Joe, parking on Camellia Lane and then reading a text on his iPhone. "But I just heard back from Adelia's butler, and he says Scooter and Mary did get divorced over the summer." Joe's fingers flew over the phone with more questions in text form, and he paused for a second to read Ozzy's instant response.

"Okay, I just texted him about Scooter staying at the Merriwether house, and he replied that the Merriwethers are longtime friends of both Mrs. Earle and the Simmons family, and that Scooter probably has an open invitation to stay at their house."

Indeed, as we watched from our spot behind some spruce trees, Scooter used his flashlight app on his phone to light his way to the front door, where he jauntily inserted a key and went inside. Within seconds, we could see a large TV come on. Through a linen curtain, we could see the unmistakable form of Scooter pouring himself a large Scotch.

"I knew Scooter was just pretending to be a one-glass-of-wine guy!" Bootsie announced from the backseat. "Look, he's going back for a refill already."

"Good thing Scotch doesn't go bad," observed Joe. "That house has been empty for, like, a year and a half. Probably pretty dusty in there, too."

"Leena from the Pack-N-Ship has a job checking the house and dusting once a week," Bootsie informed us. How Bootsie knows this kind of info is a mystery, but she always does.

"Scooter is draining Mariellen's bar," said Holly, as the blazer-clad form went back for another large glug of whiskey.

"I have to go peepee," said Gerda. "Sorry if that is too much information."

"Me too!" echoed Sophie.

"You need to hold it," Joe told them. "And hand me that bottle again. Yeah, I know, these woods are probably filled with police who are about to bust me for car drinking."

At that moment, a loud rap came on the driver's window, and we all froze, Joe with bottle upside down and aiming into his throat.

"Hi there," said Officer Walt. "I see that the driver of this SUV isn't making great decisions about mixing alcohol and driving tonight. What are you doing parked back here, anyway?"

Chapter Ten

"Joe, you need Uber account," Gerda said darkly. "I might have failed my permit test three times, but you would not pass sobriety exam."

"What are you doing here, Walt?" countered Bootsie a minute later, after Joe had stowed the booze back in its carton. "Are you watching Scooter Simmons, too? Because he's a total crook, if that's what you've heard."

"I don't have to tell you why I'm here, but why are you sitting out here spying on Simmons?" Officer Walt returned mildly. "Because you're on private property, and I had an e-mail from Lilly Merriwether that an old family friend was going to be staying at her mom's house this week, and not to worry if I saw some lights on and a car here. Also," he added, "I like to check in here every week or so as a favor to Lilly."

"We're trying to help out Eula Morris," Bootsie told him. "She doesn't know what a shyster her new boyfriend is. Just look at him!" she said, indicating Scooter's outline through the curtains. "The blue blazer and the fancy loafers scream 'guilty'!"

"He would be more comfortable in a tracksuit while relaxing watching television," agreed Gerda from the backseat.

"The point is, Walt, that we're pretty sure Scooter Simmons stole something valuable from Eula," Holly told the officer, "and since what he swiped from his sort-of-girlfriend was something she neglected to declare at customs, we promised her we wouldn't share the details with you."

"Eula hasn't reported anything missing," Walt replied. "So let's call it a night."

"I'LL DRIVE," I offered, and Joe and I exchanged places and I followed Walt's car out of the driveway and down Camellia Lane. "I'll drop everyone off and bring your car back in the morning, okay, Joe?"

"Absolutely not," he said. "Just pull into Holly's driveway, wait five minutes, and then go back to Mariellen's house. This suitcase snatch is going down tonight."

Everyone else thought this was a great idea, so 11:45 saw us back in the same grove of spruce trees. For my part, I felt extremely nervous. If Walt came back, how would I explain to John that I'd been arrested breaking into his ex-mother-in-law's house? That didn't sound good. Lilly Merriwether might think I had some weird obsession with her, too, which isn't all that far from the truth—but that manifests itself more with worrying that she'll move back here. To that end, I occasionally ask John how his ex is doing. (In a casual way, of course.) Getting caught jimmying a lock to wander around at midnight in Lilly's mom's house would definitely throw a wrench into my relationship with John.

"What do you think is the most vulnerable door in the house?" Bootsie asked me and Holly, since the three of us have been inside

Mariellen's house before—Holly and Bootsie for garden tour parties, and myself at gunpoint when Mariellen went cuckoo two summers ago and almost killed me, my neighbors the Bests, and Waffles.

"I'm thinking we go through the door to Mariellen's library," Bootsie said. "The farm-style Dutch door. Probably will take me less than a minute to open." With this, she waved her trusty barrette, which is her tool of choice for locked doors and cabinets. Bootsie's technique was honed as a teen when her parents attempted to bar her and Chip from their liquor cabinet with a simple padlock, which she quickly mastered the art of opening with a bobby pin.

"I'm ready!" said Joe, way too loudly.

"You are too drunk to be burglar," Gerda told him. "You must stay in car."

Terrified at the prospect of returning to the scene of my almost-demise, but more scared to let Bootsie and Gerda head in *a deux*, since both tend to go rogue, I followed the two six-foot blondes toward the farm door that leads to Mariellen's fancy library. Bootsie jiggled the hair accessory in the lock for about ten seconds, and the door popped open. No alarm sounded, probably because Lilly had remotely disabled it for her houseguest.

It was dark inside the elegant Colonial home, but a single front hall sconce lent minimal illumination to the library. I shook in my fake Uggs as I saw the monogrammed cushions, the hot-pink toile upholstery, and tons of photos of the gorgeous Lilly and Norman, Mariellen's beloved horse! Leena had been taking her dusting duties seriously, I noticed, since the house looked spotless and in good order.

The sound of gentle, boozy snoring came from the living room, and the three of us paused, not sure which way to direct our search.

"You think the Samsonite is in living room with Scooter? Or, like, hidden in kitchen cupboards under sacks of flour?" whispered Gerda.

"I'm thinking Scooter would keep it near him," hissed Bootsie. "And every once in a while, he probably flips the suitcase open just to admire all that gold. Since he's asleep, you go in and roll out the Samsonite, Kristin."

"What?" I said, shocked. "I'm not going into the living room all by myself!"

"I do not have a light tread," said Gerda, "so I stay here. Don't trip in those large boots, though," she told me, giving my almost-Uggs a withering glance. "There are many knickknacks, figurines, and lamps that could cause you to fall over."

I gave up, tiptoed (if you can tiptoe in giant rubber-soled boots) down the hallway, from which vantage point I immediately saw the suitcase! It was indeed at Scooter's feet, but luckily appeared to be latched, closed, and ready to roll.

I reached next to the slumbering lawyer—grasping the Samsonite's handle and gently guiding it into the hall. The noise from its squeaky new wheels sounded deafening, and Bootsie clearly agreed, because she grabbed the piece of luggage, which weighed a ton, and we made a break for it through the library's Dutch door.

"Did you hear something?" I hissed as we all jumped into the car, with me in the driver's seat, and Bootsie next to me, cradling the Samsonite on her lap. "Maybe Scooter saw us!" I said, two-wheeling out of the driveway and down Camellia Lane.

"He was asleep! He couldn't have seen us. And, even if he pretty much knows it was us, he can't call the police to report that we grabbed what he already stole," said Bootsie.

"What if he tells Eula?" I asked. "Oh, wait, he'll have the same problem. He can't admit that we broke in unless he confesses to grabbing her gold-filled luggage."

"He is screwed. Also, that was good time," said Gerda. "I enjoy stealing this large luggage item."

"It was kind of fun," agreed Bootsie. "Anyone have any idea where we can put the bag for a few days?"

"Wait—aren't we going to return it to Eula?" I asked, pulling over in front of Holly's driveway. "We need to tell her that her new boyfriend robbed her!"

"Eventually we'll return the Samsonite." Joe shrugged. "But we could torture Eula for, say, seventy-two hours thinking it's still missing. After that, I guess we should tell her Scooter isn't a good guy," he added reluctantly.

"I agree to tell Eula this information about her terrible boyfriend," Gerda said solemnly. "She claims she hasn't gotten naked with the guy yet, and we can save her from that indignity."

"Maybe we can find Eula a new boyfriend," I mused, feeling a bit bad for our nemesis. Until I met John, I was spectacularly unlucky in love myself, and it seemed sad that Eula had literally won the lottery but still was stuck with a terrible guy.

Holly stared at me with disdain. "We already got her a Powerball win," she said finally. "She's lucky that we're bothering to tell her that Scooter is a loser. Anyway, I like the idea of hiding the suitcase somewhere to ruin Eula's week."

"I have idea. We should put suitcase in this one's antiques store," Gerda intoned, nodding at me. "Lot of junk in her storage room. No one look there."

I started to protest that this was a bad idea, and that The Striped Awning was about to start hosting twice-a-week holiday poker parties and things were already a little messier than I'd like, given that it was the busiest shopping month of the year, but no one was listening. Gerda was still talking, and had a look of evil happiness on her face.

"Plus, I have great idea," Gerda added triumphantly. "You know how we supposed to get one gold brick for finding suitcase? I have better idea.

"Maybe we keep four of the gold bricks and we tell this Eula girl that's all that we found inside suitcase. Bingo, we make ton of cash for ourselves and I finally move out of Sophie's house!"

Chapter Eleven

THE VODKA WAS flowing when Waffles and I got to Holly's house at 9 a.m. the next morning. Gerda was tapping at Chip's computer, for which she hadn't yet figured out the password. The Colketts were helping Sophie brainstorm fun ideas for free food and drinks at the town festival.

The landscape designers were pushing for a Christmassy Bloody Mary bar at the gazebo, which Gerda was obviously against. Sophie, who'd been tasting the drinks the Colketts were stirring up, was singing "It's Beginning to Look a Lot Like Christmas." Martha was flipping Havarti-and-spinach omelettes for the talented but boozy decorators, which was probably good because both Tom and Tim were midway through what looked like their third drink, and Holly was using her Uber app to summon Jared in his borrowed vehicle.

"We're heading out on the brisket boondoggle in fifteen minutes," said Tim Colkett. "We only have five more days to find the mysterious barbecue shack near Wilmington, Delaware."

"I think it's down by the beach," Tom told him. "That's nowhere near Wilmington. Or maybe it's close to Georgetown, Delaware? Didn't we go there once for a farmhouse table? Anyway, so far we've got Jared driving, Gerda along as Google Maps navigator, and Bootsie just because she wants to come."

"Yes, but I have my shift at Maison de Booze from 2 p.m. until 6," Gerda informed them. "And I am still trying to crack the password on Chip's computer. So this trip cannot include, like, seventeen stops at antiques stores, which has been my experience on previous excursions with you guys."

"We're steering for steer! We're pulling for pork!" Tim assured her. "This is a totally food-focused road trip."

"I wish I could go, but I'm gonna be warming up my vocal cords for my cabaret tonight!" Sophie said. "You guys have your instrumentals all set, right?" she asked the Colketts.

"We know every song!" they reassured her.

"Your road trip sounds like fun," said Holly, "but I've got to go get Howard's mom's holiday gift. I can't put it off any longer. Lemieux the Jeweler is having a sale, and his mother likes nothing more than a silver tabletop ornamental bird."

I perked up at this, having a passion for anything in the avian decorative-object family myself. The handmade birds at the upscale gift shop in question were absolutely gorgeous: lifelike, feathered, delicate, birdy creatures that made a holiday table look super-festive. They were also very pricey, so I limited my enjoyment of them to driving by the Lemieux windows and admiring them from my car. Lemieux is the kind of place where one wrong step or awkward elbow movement could topple a Bernardaud salad bowl that would set you back three hundred dollars.

"Lemieux the Jeweler! I love that guy!" shrieked Sophie. "Ya ever been there, Kristin? It's that place over by Chip's golf store where all the walls are lined in suede—or maybe it's Ultrasuede—anyway, they have to buzz you in, and then you get handed champagne and they start bringing out giant diamonds! And, like, mini-quiches and Brie on crackers!"

"You're going to buy your hubby's mom a sterling silver swan when you could get her a fancy bracelet?" Tim Colkett asked Holly, as Bootsie and Joe walked in and took advantage of the Blood Mary bar.

"Trust me, the only way to get Howard's mom to break a smile is to get her a silver pheasant, chicken, or owl from the Lemieuxs," Holly informed him.

"She'll love it!" I said. Obviously, the Colketts and Holly weren't fans of bird decor, though. They all looked depressed.

"Well, you're missing out, because the Lemieuxs are originally from France, and they have a real good-looking son," Sophie told us. "This guy is basically a movie star. Picture Orlando Bloom meets Colin Firth meets Matt Bomer, and you're almost getting the picture."

"You won't be buying anything for yourself at this expensive shop, will you?" Gerda demanded of Holly. "Because you told me not to let you buy jewelry, shoes, boots, and clutch handbags for all of December. You had two glasses of wine at Sophie's post-Thanksgiving brunch and admitted you bought seven pairs of ankle booties that morning."

Holly looked stressed, but kept her composure. "Gerda, you're such a hoot!" she said with a little laugh. "I haven't even been tempted by the Lemieuxs 1930s vintage pendants or the Liz Taylor-esque bracelet with the diamond starburst pattern that I might possibly buy once this month is over."

"Well, let me at the jewelry!" Sophie said. "Because other than my budding cabaret career, I'm real depressed. Well, that and decorating town square and planning the festival, which we need to do Monday, by the way. The town holiday decorations are in that police station which is right near the Lemieuxs, so I'll stop in and see what's in there today," Sophie told Gerda and the Colketts.

"Maybe decking out the town square will make me feel better," Sophie added sadly. "Although mostly, the gnomes just remind me that last year, our first holiday together, my ex–Honey Bunny over there and I woke up to a gorgeous snowfall and had an argument over what color to paint my powder room. Then we made up and had mimosas and French toast. It was so romantic. Until we went for a walk, and Joe saw some gnomes displayed over by the luncheonette. We had to turn around, because he said those little smiling faces and chubby bodies and pointed red hats gave him nightmares worse than Krampus." Here, she aimed a pout at Joe, who shrugged.

"I don't do gnomes," he told her, pronging a forkful of the omelet Martha had just cooked for him.

"I cannot understand this attitude! Sophie, working with the gnomes tomorrow will cheer you up," promised Gerda. "There is no way that you can be sad with the adorable small figures in pointy hats peeking out from corners around the village. They are treasured holiday tradition."

Just then, a honk sounded outside in Holly's driveway. It was Jared in his parents' black Yukon. "Uber is here, as driven by Jared," announced Gerda.

"Let's get our brisket on! Grab some Clif Bars and let's go!" screamed Bootsie, herding her group out the door.

"I can only hope they go off-course and wind up at a spare-rib shack in Maryland by mistake," sighed Holly tragically, once we'd heard the Yukon zoom away. "My dream is that Gerda will miss her shift at the Maison. Every day I hope she can't come in, but she never gets sick!

"I don't know how to tell Gerda this, but she's not as welcoming as I'd like to customers," added Holly. "She's great at moving around huge crates of wine, and I love how organized she is, but it's the holidays, when I should be selling pricey vintages out the wazoo.

"I mean, she's even been limiting the Binghams to, like, two sips of wine at tastings, and she told Leena that too much free Brie would give her a spare tire and a muffin top. It doesn't create the breezy, fun vibe I was hoping for."

"I hate to say it," Joe offered dispiritedly, "because I hate Gerda, but she's great at her Pilates and aerobics classes. Wine—no. Squats and core strengthening—yes."

"I told her that, too!" Holly said, agitated. "But she said she needs more space than Le Spa can give her if she's going to expand her gym business."

"You need to get her out of the wine shop if you're ever going to break even on that place," observed Joe. "She's not exactly easy to get rid of, though. Look at how long she's been living with Sophie." He paused for a minute, chin in hand, which signified serious thought.

"Your only hope is a project that will get her so busy that she doesn't have time for Maison de Booze. She needs to be full-time at Pilates."

"Gerda can't offer more classes," Holly told him. "Le Spa doesn't want her there ten hours a day. She's mornings-only there."

"What about renovating that outbuilding next to your wine store and turning it into a gym that Gerda can run?" I suggested, gathering up my stuff and attempting to aim Waffles for the door—no easy task, because Martha had made him an omelette, too, which he'd eaten with gusto, and he was now asleep on the kitchen floor.

"That's perfect!" Holly said. "People can go through one of Gerda's hellish classes and come right over to Maison de Booze for some sauvignon blanc! Obviously everyone's going to need a lot of alcohol after the physical and emotional pain Gerda likes to inflict.

"You can redo the place for me and Gerda!" she told Joe. "She likes all white walls and blond wood floors. I'll order all the machines and equipment, and you handle the renovations and do an amazing marble lobby with front desk and changing room with gorgeous orchids everywhere and a steam room. That won't take long to do, right?"

"If you're willing to pay overtime, it won't," Joe informed her.

"Can you get it done in three weeks?"

"That's a lot of overtime," he said, starting to run numbers on his iPhone calculator, his eye taking on a signature gleam that reflected a new and pricey project.

"Of course, I'll give you a friends-and-family discount on my design fee," Joe said, still entering numbers, "but given the fact that I'm pretty sure that old barn, or whatever it is, hasn't been touched since 1927, this could get expensive. I'm heading over there now to look around a little, but given that there's likely no plumbing, wiring, heat, and the roof has sizable holes in it, I'm thinking six weeks and a mid-February opening, with a team of four guys working fourteen-hour days."

"Great!" said Holly. "And I just had a genius idea, let's add Gerda to your construction team, which will keep her out of the wine store. Can your guys start tomorrow?"

Chapter Twelve

"I THOUGHT THE brisket place was down Route 912, which leads to a bunch of farm towns where we get buy roses and hydrangeas in the summer," Tim Colkett explained when he, Tom, and Bootsie stopped by The Striped Awning at 5:45 that afternoon. "Plus, there are some great discount liquor places down there."

"And there's a really good Ralph Lauren outlet there, too," Tom added. "Plus, Delaware has no sales tax."

"Let me speed this story up: The BBQ was a bust," Bootsie said. "We saw donut places, a fried-chicken stand, and crab shacks. No BBQ. I'm starting to think maybe you guys were in another state when you went to this place—if you really did even have this supposed sandwich."

"I guess it's possible that this happened in another part of this beautiful country of ours," agreed Tom. "Maybe this happened last summer when we were in Georgia on that bench-buying trip? Or there was that weekend we went to Maine. Do they have barbecue up there?"

"Anyway," said Tim, "finally we turned around and decided to make a quick run into Ralph Lauren, which I was thinking might be a good place for Gerda to grab a new outfit for the cabaret tonight."

"I think she'd look good in a mini and boots," offered Tom Colkett. "Sporty is her thing, I know, but Gerda in a mini would have a really fun vibe. I'd pair it with a turtleneck."

"So Tom was trying on some polos, and I was trying on some tennis skirts, because Ralph makes really good ones, when who do I see holding three bow ties, a navy blazer, and a striped pink shirt, waiting to check out, but Scooter!" Bootsie said.

Bootsie recounted that Scooter had been focused on his purchases, and had paid and climbed into the backseat of a black SUV, which had then sped up I-95 toward the airport. While Jared and the Colketts waited outside, Bootsie went into the ticketing area and saw Scooter head to a Windsong Airlines desk, which runs four flights a day to Miami.

"I'm working on a theory that Scooter's involved in the Chip kidnapping!" Bootsie said. "Miami is close to the Florida Keys, and that means the L'Etoile hotel deal is blowing up and we need to be there! Well, probably, since Gerda hasn't gotten into Chip's e-mails yet. But I'm convinced Scooter's somehow involved in the Chip debacle.

"So I'm leaving tomorrow at 8 a.m. for Swan Key via Miami, since obviously we can't miss Sophie's cabaret. Let me call Holly, so she can use some of her frequent flyer miles to book the rest of you on the same flight."

"You can leave us out, doll," Tom Colkett told Bootsie. "Sounds fun, but we're gonna be tired after the cabaret, and we still gotta find that guy with the brisket, so we'll be heading back to Delaware this weekend."

I started protesting that I, too, wanted to be left out, but Bootsie had already reached Holly, who immediately agreed, and added that Waffles could stay at her house with Martha.

Just then, Joe showed up. "I got your text about Florida," he told Bootsie. "I'm in! I actually need to check in on Adelia Earle's cottage's new shower rod anyway, so this works out great.

"So, when are we going to break the news to Eula about Scooter taking off for Miami?" he said, a hint of evil glee in his face. "Not that I don't feel a *little* bad for her," he added.

"I guess we could do it tonight at the cabaret," Bootsie told him, consulting her watch. "I need to leave soon to pick up Gerda at Maison de Booze. Sophie's home getting ready for her performance, and she asked me to give Gerda a ride back to her house so Gerda can lead her through her vocal warm-ups."

"You know," Joe said pensively, "maybe we should give Eula back the gold bars right now and wind up this Samsonite saga. I mean, after we take our own gold brick as reward, which I'm planning to hide buried in some mulch in Holly's front yard until we can figure out how to sell it without getting taxed. Anyway, let's pick up Gerda, then take the suitcase over to Eula's house."

"Good idea," I agreed, anxious to have the valuable items far away from The Striped Awning, and preferably in a bank vault somewhere.

"Great, let's grab the luggage and go," agreed Bootsie.

"We're out of here," the Colketts told us, heading out the front door. "Got to change and get our keyboards and bass over to Gianni's by eight."

Joe, meanwhile, headed to the back room of my shop, where I could now hear him rummaging around. "What the fuck?" he said. "Could you have any more Windex back here? And where'd you put the suitcase?" he demanded, sticking his head back inside the sales floor from where he stood in my storage area.

"What?" I said, shocked.

"You didn't move the Samsonite?"

"I haven't gone back there today!" I said, panicked. "I've only had four customers, and they all stayed near the front of the store. No one's been in there all day!"

Bootsie, Joe, and I spent the next fifteen minutes looking through every inch of the store and back room for the missing rolling suitcase, which really only took about three minutes, since the shop's not that big and a piece of luggage is hard to hide. The suitcase was gone.

"My nine-thousand-seven-hundred-fifty-dollar windfall!" yelled Joe. "This holiday is ruined even worse than it was before, thanks to Sophie's stupid New Year's Day wedding idea, when everyone knows that's a terrible day to start something new!"

"What color was that suitcase again?" asked Bootsie suddenly. "Was it, um, blue?"

Joe and I both stared at her.

"Why are you asking that?" Joe demanded suspiciously.

"Well, the Colketts and I had a couple of beers in Delaware before we got to the Ralph Lauren outlet, and come to think of it, I think when Scooter got dropped off at the airport, he might have had a blue rollerboard with him," Bootsie said nonchalantly. "Huh. I guess I didn't realize it was the same one he took from Eula."

"Yes, the missing Samsonite was *blue*," screamed Joe. "It was the thirty-inch Black Label Firelite spinner in deep blue, to be exact. Scooter must have broken in here last night and stolen back Eula's gold!"

"WE'RE GOING TO have to grill Eula about what she knows that could help lead us to Scooter, and the suitcase, and thereby find Chip," said Bootsie.

She and Joe were too upset to drive—Bootsie seemed slightly more devastated about the suitcase than she had when Chip had disappeared, which I didn't point out—so we'd all piled into my car to pick up Gerda at work. We were now headed for Eula's house, with Waffles sitting happily in the back between Joe and Gerda, neither of whom looked especially pleased to have a panting dog as a seatmate.

"Scooter must have mentioned *something* to Eula about a hotel deal he was working on," Bootsie mused. She paused for a moment. "I'll probably enjoy telling her about Scooter and the suitcase, but I'm angry that we have to admit that someone then stole it from *us*."

I noticed that Eula's house was freshly painted, and that sometime during the fall, she'd had a lot of new holly bushes and trees planted. There were crisp new black shutters, a jaunty navy front door, and a large American flag, as well as huge, fragrant wreaths on all the windows, and lots of lush greenery surrounding the doors and windows.

"Eula!" screamed Bootsie, rapping on a French door and startling the house's owner, who was midworkout on a VersaClimber. Eula hopped off her home gym equipment and opened up.

"Did you find my suitcase?" she asked breathlessly.

"Sort of," Bootsie told her, as Joe, Gerda, Waffles, and I crowded into Eula's living room, which still had the cute new pillows and rug that Joe had decorated it with last summer as part of a scheme to gain access and search Eula's house for a missing painting.

"I did a fantastic job on this place," Joe congratulated himself.

"In two hours last summer, I took this place from hand-me-down shack to boho-chic-meets-design-within-reach." Eula shrugged off the insult, which is one of her better qualities.

Joe's dissed my own run-down cottage many times, so I've gotten used to it, but actually Eula's place was in way better shape than mine.

She must have used some of her Powerball cash to have the kitchen spruced up, too, I thought, noticing it was sheathed in sparkling white marble. A cool starburst light fixture now was hanging over the dining room table, which I don't think her aunt would have installed before she'd bequeathed the place to Eula.

"I like this house," announced Gerda, giving an appreciative nod to the living room's high ceiling, large fireplace, and mullioned windows. "This puts me in mind of small mountain houses in Austria."

"Yeah, it's cute," agreed Eula. "But I'm thinking of buying a bigger place when I'm back from the *Palace of the Seas* trip. Something more like Holly's place."

At this, Joe perked up. I could see where he was headed: As much as he hates Eula, if she was going to buy a big old house that needed renovation, he could suddenly find a way to get along with her. For her part, though, Bootsie kept the conversation on track.

"Eula, we have some bad news," she told her bluntly. "Your boyfriend stole your suitcase. Then, we stole it from him, but he seems to have purloined your Samsonite once again. And we're not planning to recover it for you until you tell us everything Scooter blabbed to you about his current business deal in Florida."

"Scooter wouldn't do that to me!" Eula wailed. "And he didn't take my new diamond necklace, either! Oops," she added hastily, realizing she hadn't mentioned missing jewelry to us before.

"I can't find a few pieces of jewelry I picked up on my cruise, but they're probably around here somewhere. Anyway, there's no way Scootie would do this."

"Eula, I'm telling you that we broke into the house where Scooter has been staying and found your Samsonite right next to him, and you don't think he stole it?"

"One thing I don't understand," I said. "The night that your suitcase was stolen, you said you had dinner with Scooter. So he maybe he hired someone else to grab it?" I wondered aloud.

"I asked Channing about that," Bootsie told me. "Scooter was twenty minutes late to meet you at the restaurant that night. Plenty of time to grab that Samsonite."

Eula didn't deny this, and we could see from her sad pout that she was beginning to realize we were telling her the truth. "Maybe he was just keeping my valuables safe for me?" she ventured sadly.

We all raised our eyebrows at this, since Scooter's nothing if not sneaky.

In the one week we'd known him last January, he'd faked zoning documents, sawed down a rare and endangered oak tree, staked out a huge condo building on a protected beachfront, and slipped Klonopin into his half brother's drink.

"I'm going to level with you, Eula," Joe told her. "Normally, I'd enjoy seeing you date a guy who's known to be a total weasel, but in this case, I want my nine-thousand-seven-hundred-fifty-dollar share of your gold brick, so I need to know where Scooter told you he was going for this business meeting. Is the meeting in the Florida Keys?

"Because your new boyfriend seems to be involved with some shady business deal that has Bootsie's brother Chip in the hole for fifty thousand dollars, and Chip might lose some important body parts, namely an eyelid and all his eyelashes, if we don't help him out."

"Scooter did mention he was going to Florida for a business deal," Eula told us sadly. "It might have been in the Keys." Then she crumpled onto a new pale gray sofa, and burst into a crazy storm of tears. "I'm starting to believe you're right about Scooter! All my new diamonds that I got duty-free in Paradise Island were in the Samsonite, too, but I was too embarrassed to tell you!"

We all looked uncomfortable, and finally Bootsie broke the awkward silence.

"There's only one thing you can do, Eula, to make yourself feel better. And that one thing is to be at Gianni's in"—here she checked her watch—"less than an hour, so hurry up and get in the shower. Tonight you can enjoy an amazing cabaret starring Sophie Shields, guzzle a bunch of champagne, ogle Channing the hot chef, and tell us everything you ever heard Scooter say about a shady hotel deal in Florida!"

Chapter Thirteen

"*JINGLE BELLS*," TRILLED Sophie in a jazzy voice at 8 p.m., looking gorgeous in the silver beaded minidress that she and the Colketts had finally agreed upon. She'd perfected a little dance routine that the Colketts had "curated," as they called it, which included feet tapping, some sultry hip swivels, and a few high kicks.

"*Ji-ji-jingle bells*," chorused the Colketts from behind their instruments, with Tim on keyboards and Tom on the standup bass. They were performing the tune in the swingy big-band style of Bing Crosby and the Andrews Sisters.

"This is awesome!" whispered Bootsie. "The Colketts sound amazing, Sophie looks fantastic, and the whole vibe is totally Café Carlyle meets Fred Astaire meets Eartha Kitt!"

"*Oh, what fun it is to ride in a one-horse open sleigh!*" sang Sophie.

"*Hey!*" responded the Colketts in melodic unison, sawing away at the bass and banging on the keyboards.

Restaurant Gianni's bar area had taken on the vibe of a 1940s nightclub, I noticed, with the lights down low, candles flickering, and Christmassy decorations hung everywhere. Champagne was flowing, and the thirty-five-dollar ticket price to the cabaret included a raw bar of shrimp and lobster cocktail.

If only John were here, I thought, feeling both wistful and irked. Sure, he'd been by my side at Thanksgiving, but that was weeks ago. Maybe Mike Woodford would be here tonight, and would get more specific about the possible dinner date he'd mentioned. That would show John!

"Look, there's the handsome jeweler Pierre Lemieux," said Holly. "He just sent Sophie a glass of champagne to sip on her break between songs!" She looked meaningfully at Joe, who cast his eyes toward the kitchen and swigged some Scotch. "Maybe you should go tell Sophie that you're ready to get married, and then Pierre's champagne will go flat."

"How old is this Pierre Lemieux?" asked Gerda disapprovingly. "Looks pretty young to me."

We all eyed the handsome, dark-haired jeweler. He appeared to be about thirty, and had on a sleek navy suit that even outdid Joe in its crisp, unwrinkled perfection. He was smiling at Sophie approvingly, and gave a little whistle of approval as she finished up a soulful, meaningful, yet festive take on "Blue Christmas," with plenty of significant looks aimed at Joe.

"Younger men are the new older men," announced Holly. "Sophie might be in the market for a guy in the Lemieux age bracket."

"She's great at working the room!" I said admiringly. "Sophie's a natural at performing."

As everyone broke into huge applause, Sophie and the Colketts took multiple bows.

"How did the bird figurines work out?" I asked Holly, as Sophie walked over to where our group sat with a miserable Eula Morris. Mike, I noted sadly, was nowhere to be seen.

"It wasn't as successful as we hoped," said Holly.

"It was real scary!" shrieked Sophie, drying off a little sheen of perspiration with a starched white napkin.

"Right after we got there, a guy came in and robbed the Lemieuxs!"

Sophie explained that Holly had been about to examine some sterling figurines of grouse and Sophie herself had been about to layer on a few tennis bracelets, when all of a sudden, the Lemieux front door had been thrown open, and a guy in a mask and nondescript jeans and sneakers had come in. He'd had a gun and a note demanding that everything in the front display cases be handed over. Within seconds, he'd grabbed bracelets, an antique starburst pendant, and a few rings from the front display cases, but the alarm was going off like crazy. Within seconds, the guy was gone, having never spoken.

"And he moved like a robot," Sophie said. "He had gloves on, a scarf, and his mask was one of those super-creepy ones that go all the way over the head and down to the shirt collar, so you can't see anything about the person underneath!"

"What kind of mask was it?" demanded Bootsie. "I need to know this stuff for the Gazette!"

"It was—get this—a Krampus mask!" shrieked Sophie. "And it was scary as heck! But you can forget your newspaper story. This one's already on the Philly papers' Web sites and everything. Not only was Officer Walt called in by the Lemieuxs, but your editor in chief showed up. He said he was writing this story himself, and it's gonna be front page tomorrow."

"What time was this?" I asked. "Could it have been Scooter

dressed as Krampus? Because he was shopping at a Ralph Lauren outlet at, like, lunchtime, and then headed for the airport at 12:45."

"You know what—it was early, maybe 10:15 a.m., so maybe Krampus *was* Scooter!" mused Sophie. "I mean, I didn't pick up on a resemblance, but that gives him time to get down to Delaware, shop, and hit the airport!"

"By the way, Gerda, we have an early holiday present for you," Holly told her. "Your own gym. Joe's going to completely remodel the barn next to the wine store so you can have two Pilates rooms, a gym, and a steam room."

Gerda broke into one of her once-a-year smiles. "Merry Christmas to me!" she said. "This is a very welcome gift which will keep on giving via greater fitness for this village! Thank you in a very big way." She thought for a moment. "This could be the year I expand into an empire of Pilates for more out-of-shape Americans. Also, I am thinking of way to convince Eula to sell me her cottage, which is my ideal home."

Eula, for her part, ignored Gerda's informal offer on her house. She was still calling and texting Scooter, but couldn't reach him.

"Hon, that guy flew the coop," Tim Colkett told Eula when the Colketts joined our group. "We saw him heading into the airport."

"He's gonzo," seconded Tom. "He flew out of town right after he left the Ralph Lauren outfit, and this one"—here, he pointed to Bootsie—"trailed him into the check-in area, where he went to the Windsong Airline desk, and you know they only fly to Florida."

"Plus, he stole your suitcase—twice," Bootsie pointed out.

I felt badly for Eula, honestly. I had really started to think Scooter might have been The One for her. Scooter had the charm and manners to make her happy. If only he had sneaked the suitcase back into her house last night, the two could have resumed their romance, and the holidays would be back on track. Plus, an upbeat, in-love Eula would probably rarely come back to town! She'd be too busy wandering Rome or St. Tropez on Scooter's arm to visit, and Holly and Joe could go off their anxiety medication, and all the town festivals, cabarets (not that those happened much), and events would be Eula-free.

"You're better off without Scooter," Joe told Eula, surprising me with this relatively sympathetic response. I was even more shocked when he grabbed the bottle of wine he'd ordered for us, lit up one of the Colketts' Marlboro Silvers—which isn't legal to smoke inside, but it didn't seem like Channing and Jessica were enforcing Clean Indoor Air Act laws tonight—and plunked himself down between Tom and Tim and next to Eula.

"I guess so," agreed Eula, pouring herself more wine. "I really thought Scooter was perfect for me," she said, dabbing at her eyes with a napkin, "but he *was* kind of secretive."

"He checked your Samsonite rollerboard to Miami, doll," Tim Colkett told her. "That's more than secretive."

Meanwhile Sophie was watching, mouth agape, as Joe listened to Eula's tale of love gone wrong.

"Are you freaking kiddin' me?" she finally exploded. "Joe, how dare you sit with Eula on my big night? And, no offense, Eula, but you're wearing a gold Roberto Cavalli lace minidress, and everyone knows metallics are my signature color!"

"Sophie, have a drink with me," said Pierre Lemieux, approaching our table with soulful eyes gazing at the newly minted cabaret star. "I get you a bottle of champagne. You are ten times more beautiful than Eula here! She has nothing on Sophie Shields!"

"Thanks, Pierre," Sophie said gratefully. "Sure, top off my glass. And let's do a shot of Patrón. What the heck!"

Holly and I exchanged worried glances, since Sophie isn't a big drinker.

"We're going to take Sophie home, Pierre, but thanks," Holly told him, quickly extricating Sophie from the jeweler and steering her toward the exit. "You're so thoughtful, though!"

"What about Joe?" I whispered, as we inserted Sophie into her coat. "Shouldn't we drive him home? He looks kind of tipsy."

"I'm gonna go say good-bye to the Colketts and Jessica," Sophie told us, heading for the bar, which had turned into an illegal smokers' area.

"Stay away from Pierre!" Holly ordered her. "Do *not* leave the bar area and disappear with a thirty-year-old French jeweler!"

"Look!" said Bootsie. Eula and Joe had their heads together, and suddenly the unlikely pair got up and headed for the door.

"It's weird that Joe's leaving with Eula, but she doesn't seem drunk, so I guess it's okay for her to be driving," I said. "Luckily, Sophie didn't see them go off together. She's over there puffing on a cigarette, which is also strange, because Sophie doesn't smoke."

"Oh my gosh, Joe is gonna get some Eula lovin'!" exploded Bootsie. "This goes against every instinct he's ever had!"

"Shhhh!" I told her. "Sophie can't know about Joe leaving with Eula! Pipe down, or she'll hear you. Luckily, she and the Colketts are singing 'One for My Baby,' which isn't a good idea, because that song is depressing. Uh-oh, now she's singing and smoking at the same time."

Sophie started coughing, and while the Colketts grabbed her Marlboro Silver and stubbed it out while they patted her on the back, Sophie suddenly appeared to sober up and pointed to a back corner of Gianni's main dining room.

"Hey, wait a minute. I recognize that white button-down shirt, the navy blue sweater, the shaggy hair, and the sneakers," shrieked Sophie. "That's the evil Santa who shot at me and drove the getaway car for the guy who threatened Chip!"

The guy in the white shirt looked scared, scrambled to his feet, and made for the exit at a dead run, but he was too late.

"Come on, Gerda, let's get him!" yelled Bootsie.

Chapter Fourteen

"WHERE'S MY BROTHER?" demanded Bootsie, after she and Gerda had escorted the erstwhile Santa back to his table. "And what are you doing here, anyway, and what's your name? Are you a cabaret fan?"

"I'm not supposed to say anything!" the guy told her. We all glared at him, and I was surprised to notice he looked about seventeen years old. "My name's Dave. This is just a part-time job for me. I don't know much, honestly!"

"You know what?" Bootsie told him. "I'm getting angry now." She jumped up and lunged at the terrified Dave, seizing him by the top of his ear and twisting the soft, tender flesh in a Delaney family signature move.

"Ow!" screamed Dave. "Ouch! Make it stop!" He started dancing around in pain with Bootsie hanging on to his ear. "Your brother's in Florida! He's supposed to be paying back some businessmen on a fake resort scam. I mean, from what I hear, there's an actual hotel called L'Etoile, but it's nothing like what they sold investors on."

Bootsie ordered Dave to sit and she let go of his ear, which he rubbed at energetically.

"I don't think your brother really knew what he was getting into, and was supposed to find more people to scam with the deal, but instead he backed out. I work part-time as a driver for a group of businessmen in Jersey who have a less-than-legal construction business, as well as run some gambling and tobacco operations on the side.

"Anyway, I listen while I drive," admitted Dave. "Last week, I was driving this guy Pete Penworthy around Trenton when he came up from Florida for some meetings. Pete said a friend of his wanted to scare his ex-wife and wanted to arrange a drive-by shooting, but just to hit, like, her front steps or a shrub. I wasn't supposed to actually shoot that close to you, Mrs. Shields, but I was so nervous that my hand shook and I got your purse by mistake!" he told Sophie apologetically. "You're okay, though, right?"

"I'm okay, but my handbag isn't!" she informed him.

"You not too good at this line of work," Gerda told Dave. "Maybe you need to look for different job."

"Listen, lady, I'm saving up to finish up my college degree, and this pays better than jobs at the mall and the gas station. What am I supposed to do?"

"So what happened with the threatening note tied to a golf club and thrown into Chip's truck?" I asked him.

"Mr. Penworthy called from Florida and told me to drive one of his henchmen to shake up Chip," the guy told us. "I didn't mess that job up," he added, looking around with some pride.

"How dare you scare my brother!" Bootsie said, straightening up into her full height and looming over Dave, looking as menacing as a country-club tennis champ who's skilled at noogies can—which seemed to have the desired effect, as he shrank into his seat.

"Listen, lady, I don't do actual hurting of people," protested Dave. "Anyway, today I drove another friend of Mr. Penworthy's to do some outlet shopping in Delaware and then to the airport. I think he's got something to do with the money that Chip owes Mr. P."

"I knew Scooter was in on this!" screamed Bootsie. "That guy stole a ton of valuables from a friend of ours. Well, not a friend, because we don't like her. Anyway, then he stole this stuff back from us."

"I heard about that," Dave told her. "That guy Scooter bragged to me that he pretended to be asleep when you grabbed the suitcase from the house he was staying in. But he followed you people back to some dinky antiques store with the lights off on his BMW, and stuck a credit card between the doorframe and the doorknob and walked right in. He said the lock was older than dirt, and provided zero security."

"I told you to get better locks!" Bootsie yelled at me.

"It wasn't my idea to hide ridiculously valuable items behind my mops and Windex!" I told her.

"Unfortunately, Scooter dented his pricey rental car on the way back from the antiques store to the house where he was staying, because he'd had a lot of Scotch, so he had to get the BMW towed back to Avis," Dave continued. "Which is how I ended up waiting outside while he robbed that jewelry store today dressed as Krampus.

"Oops!" Dave added. "I wasn't supposed to mention that to anyone. And then I had to drive him to Delaware and to the airport today." He paused. "What was in that suitcase, anyway? He was real secretive about it."

"Shut up," Bootsie ordered him.

"How old are you?" asked Gerda. "You look like you not completely through puberty yet."

"I'm twenty-one," Dave said proudly. "Legally able to hit the bars and liquor stores."

"If I were you, I wouldn't drink," said Gerda grimly. "You might not be finished growing yet, and alcohol gonna stunt you. Plus, you aren't good at your job already. Drinking gonna make you even worse."

"Maybe it'll make him better at being a goombah," offered Bootsie. "Loosen him up a little."

It seemed like Bootsie was now defending the guy who'd shot her brother's delivery truck, and I sensed it was time to head home.

"One thing I should tell you, Mrs. Shields," Dave said, preparing to leave and lowering his voice as he headed for the door. "I hear your ex is still in love with you, but he just invited his girlfriend Diana-Maria to move into your old house with him. I just thought you should know!"

"That makes me super-mad!" shrieked Sophie. "We haven't even finished up negotiating the divorce terms!"

Diana-Maria was the ex-inamorata of a guy named Lobster Phil LaMonte, a crony of Sophie and Barclay from their Jersey days. Like most women, Sophie wasn't okay with her ex dating, even though she had been the one who walked out on Barclay.

"So why did you come to this restaurant tonight?" asked Gerda. "You supposed to be shooting someone again, or what?"

Dave paused, embarrassed. "I heard Mrs. Shields was doing a show here," he mumbled. "And I have a little crush on her."

"Aw!" said Sophie. "That's real sweet. I forgive you about the purse!"

"That's cute," Bootsie told Dave. "And guess what? We're all heading to Florida tomorrow to find Chip, and you're coming with us. In fact, we can offer you in exchange for Chip," she added, inspired.

"I've never been to Florida!" said Dave, excited. "But I don't think they'll swap me for Chip. I'm pretty sure I'm fired over the purse-shooting incident."

"Well, you're going anyway," said Bootsie. "I'm sending you back to Sophie's house. Gerda here will watch over you all night until you get on the plane with us tomorrow morning. What's your last name?" she asked, whipping out her phone to buy him a ticket.

"It's Conover," Dave told her, looking alarmed at the thought of being guarded by Gerda.

"My mom's expecting me home by twelve-thirty tonight, and I live an hour away, way up by Rumson, and I don't have any clothes with me!"

"Too bad," Bootsie told him. "Tell your mom you got a new job that's taking you out of town for a couple days. We'll get you some shorts and polos in the Miami airport tomorrow."

"And some loafers," added Gerda. "Those high-top sneakers are not suitable for a man aged twenty-one."

"Hand over your phone, Dave," Bootsie told him. "You'll get it back when we're done in Florida. Welcome to the Delaney-McElvoy family, kid. You're working for me now!"

Chapter Fifteen

THE NEXT DAY, 11:30 a.m. saw us cruising south on U.S. Route 1 toward Swan Key, Florida. We'd gotten the 8 a.m. flight out of Philly, landed in Miami at 10:25, and Sophie and Holly had quickly hit the airport Thomas Pink, Ron Jon, and Johnston & Murphy stores for some clothes for Dave. Then we'd gone to the rental car pickup, where Joe, who's a self-proclaimed expert at getting the best and coolest cars from rental clerks at rock-bottom prices, had reserved a special tricked-out Cadillac SUV that seated seven, which would allow all of us, plus Chip if we successfully rescued him, to roam South Florida in roomy comfort.

Unfortunately, the clerk told us, a crew from the *Today Show* en route to an interview with Pitbull had gotten there ten minutes earlier and rented the giant Cadillac.

We were shown to a dented minivan, where a hungover Joe took the wheel as we passed margarita bars, surfboard shops, and bikini barns. I called Martha and heard that Waffles had enjoyed some scrambled eggs, wandered around Holly's yard for ten minutes, and was now asleep on a cozy cashmere blanket.

"The dog is having a better day than we are," said Joe, looking completely depressed despite the festive scenery and palm trees we were passing. Before falling asleep on the plane, he'd confessed to Holly and me to waking up at 5 a.m. in Eula's bed, but said that he'd been on top of Eula's crisp new bedding, and that his shirt had been rumpled and untucked, but he'd been fully dressed.

Luckily, he'd packed for Florida before the cabaret, and his duffel had been duly loaded into Bootsie's car before we swung by Eula's house to pick him up 5:15 a.m. and headed for the airport. It was rare to see Joe unshaven—although the bloodshot eyes and slightly shaky hands weren't all that uncommon after a big night, I thought to myself.

Anyway, as he drove south, Joe was starting to look a lot better. Unfortunately, Sophie had figured out where Joe had spent the night, even though we'd picked her, Gerda, and Dave up last on the airport run. Needless to say, Sophie was devastated, and was mopping up tears with a Starbucks napkin she'd found in her purse.

Bootsie was next to Joe in the front seat, with Holly and Gerda in the second row; Sophie, Dave and I were in the back seating area, since Sophie said she wanted to be as far away as possible from Joe, and that since he'd had some kind of sexy interlude with Eula, she'd start dating again now, too. Today, if possible.

"I brought Chip's hotel prospectus with me," said Bootsie. "Kristin's seen it, but for the rest of you need to know that L'Etoile is supposed to have a Meditation Pool, Tranquility Cabanas, and a nightclub, plus a steakhouse, a sushi bar, and a bar that has all the walls covered in glittering Swarovski crystals. There are spa concierges, cocktail consultants, and golf butlers!" Bootsie read aloud.

"Is a golf butler the same as a caddy?" Joe asked.

"This place sounds awesome!" shrieked Sophie, cheering up a little. "How much are those shares again?"

"The shares are fake," Bootsie reminded her. "You'll be buying into what Dave said is probably, like, a motel on the side of a highway."

"Speaking of hotels, what's this place Holly booked us into again for tonight?" Joe asked. "Because it sounds horrible."

"Le Vert Epinard Spa and Hotel is going to be great," said Holly. "It's on a gorgeous island right across from where Chip's fake hotel is supposed to be located. Tons of movie stars, models, and HGTV hosts have stayed at Le Vert, as insiders call it."

"Wait, I took French in high school—I know that word," Joe mused. "Epinard, it's a vegetable. It's green . . . and it's healthy . . . I'm pretty sure it's something I don't like."

"You don't like Eula, but that didn't stop ya from fooling around with her!" screamed Sophie.

"I'm seventy-eight percent sure nothing naked happened between me and Eula," groaned Joe. "I do remember her showing me a lot of pictures of the *Palace of the Seas*, and of her and Scooter, and I think she might have sobbed on my shoulder. I think I'd know if I'd made out with Eula, and I don't feel any different. That must mean something, right?"

"Le Vert Epinard means green spinach," Gerda informed us. "I work in French restaurant one summer as a teenager and one of my duties was vegetable prep. I wash, like, seven thousand bunches of epinard, and this is the reason I now prefer kale and chard."

"They named the hotel for spinach?" asked Dave. "That's real weird."

"Isn't all spinach green?" asked Bootsie. "Do they have other colors now, the way there are purple potatoes and white aspara-gus? Which, by the way, I don't get. Why would you want veg-etables to be another color?"

"Colored veggies are a chef thing," Holly told her. "Chan-ning told me once that they have to look at the same vegetables every day, and if they don't get some variety, it gets super-boring. I'm thinking most men feel the same way about their significant others, which is why I got Howard that moonshine still, which I thought would distract him from the possible monotony of being married to me. Of course, my plan didn't work out, and I'm hoping that thing isn't going to explode in the garage of whoever stole it."

"I haven't had a chance to get bored of John yet," I said mourn-fully. "Since he's always out of town in places like California."

"Le Vert Whatever grows all their own food on-site!" read Sophie, who was consulting Le Vert Epinard's Web site on her phone. "And make their own cashew cheese. Huh, I didn't know that was a food."

"Please don't say the words 'cashew cheese,'" Joe told her. "Anyway, why are we staying at this spinach place, other than the movie stars? Shouldn't we be staying right where L'Etoile and hopefully Chip are?"

"Gerda and I paid for wi-fi on the plane, and we read in the Miami newspaper that a leading society matron, one Mrs. Pete Penworthy, is a frequent guest at Le Vert Epinard," Holly informed him. "She's the wife of the guy that Dave here said is the mastermind of this hotel scam. So we called when we landed and pretended to have a message from a hair salon about Mrs. Penworthy's appoint-ment time for next week, and the hotel confirmed she's there. So the plan is that we befriend Mrs. Penworthy at Le Vert Epinard, pump her for information about Chip, and solve everything."

"That plan sounds okay, but I sense a day of starvation and anger coming my way," Joe told her. "And what if you've got a bun in the oven? You can't sustain your future baby with a sprig of organic greens. Did you take the pregnancy test yet?"

"We need to rescue Chip first," Holly informed him. "This isn't the time for a run into the nearest Walgreens. I need to be in the right mental place to find out that kind of monumental news, and an interstate in Florida isn't it. So back off!" she screamed at Joe.

"You seem real hormonal," Gerda told Holly. "Maybe you just have bad PMS."

"You think that's a problem?" said Sophie. "The Fancy Feet Square Dancers from out in Chester County just called me. Apparently they've performed on the town square every December twentieth since, like, 1940, and they're determined to square dance at 4 p.m. sharp on Monday.".

"I love the Fancy Feet!" said Bootsie. "They're fantastic. They have these great outfits. Gerda, their look is basically lederhosen. You'll feel right at home."

I knew this troupe of hoofers, actually, since several of the members were regular vendors at Stoltzfus's Flea Market, one of my favorite spots to pick up silver, paintings, and antique china to sell at The Striped Awning. While they weren't exactly Baryshnikov, the square dance troupe were a fun holiday tradition— apparently one Sophie hadn't seen in her few years of living in town.

"Fancy Feet is a misnomer," observed Joe. "They're not that fancy."

"What if you got them some new outfits?" asked Holly. "We could get the Colketts to give them some kind of cool rebranding."

"What if they were, like, human peppermint martinis for

Mistletoe and Martini Night!" shrieked Sophie. "That would be awesome! They could have peppermint-striped scarves and be all glittery and martini-ish."

"The Fancy Feet don't drink," Bootsie told her. "They won't be cocktails."

"Maybe they could be, um, Abominable Snowmen!" mused Sophie, undeterred.

"I'd turn it over to the Colketts," Holly advised. "They'll have a few drinks and come up with something that will make the square dancers better than the cast of *Hamilton*."

"Look, we need to focus on the place we're staying tonight and plan accordingly, because a couple of leaves of spinach and cheese made from nuts is about all we're going to get to eat at this place," Bootsie said, then bellowed, "Pull over, Joe! Right here, at Liquor Lou's Wholesale!"

Joe took a flying right turn, gravel spewing everywhere, and parked in front of the booze warehouse. Bootsie and Joe returned to the minivan five minutes later with two bottles of tequila, thirty Slim Jims, and four bags of Doritos Salsa Verde, which they distributed among our suitcases.

"The boat for Le Vert Epinard leaves at 1:50 p.m. sharp," said Holly icily, "and the Beach Meditation is at 2:15. So if we want to find this L'Etoile place and start looking for Chip before then, you're going to need to get this minivan moving."

Chapter Sixteen

"This is the future site of L'Etoile Resort? Where will the condos go? And the docks, the disco, the cabanas, the shops, and the two restaurants?" Bootsie demanded thirty minutes later.

We'd wound down the highway through the leafy Key Largo, past some funky waterfront restaurants that Joe loudly noted looked like the perfect place for people who actually lived fun lives to stop and get fish tacos, Key lime pie, and piña coladas, but that he was stuck with a group who would soon be eating cashew cheese and that his life was in shreds. After five miles of fishing piers, cool retro motels, and some beautiful expanses of ocean, a small sign proclaimed that we had reached Swan Key.

"Google Maps says L'Etoile Hotel is right down this lane," said Gerda dubiously, looking up from her phone at a dirt lane shaded by tall, overgrown trees as birds flew by and lizards hopped past us.

The temperature was a perfect seventy-five, and avocado and lemon trees dangled fruit all around us as we drove down the leafy driveway. Joe parked the minivan near a low arched stone wall, and we climbed out to peer past the bougainvillea at an adorable old Mediterranean-style hotel.

It was painted white with a terracotta tiled roof, a large patio, and French doors, and looked like it could accommodate a dozen or so guests.

If the place had been open for business, that is, which it clearly wasn't. The foliage was overgrown and weeds had sprouted all around the building; the place had an abandoned air. Still, it had tons of potential. "I don't get it," said Bootsie. "You're sure this is the address, Gerda?"

"This is definitely it," Gerda told her. "But this doesn't look the same as what Chip's information packet described."

"This site is gorgeous!" I said, immediately taken in by the old-world vibe. There was even a tiny putting green.

"Cute, charming, and island-y is what it definitely is," said Joe. "What it *isn't* is the site of a Dubai-meets-Vegas golf resort. This place might accommodate eight or so guest rooms, and a teeny little bistro."

"Someone could build a high-rise here," intoned Gerda. "Which would be a crime against nature, but Americans often do not take into account the appropriate scale of buildings, or things like frogs, turtles, and big fat native seals that live in Florida."

"Manatees?" said Sophie. "They're real cute! I've always wanted to hug one of them!"

"I believe most of Florida outside of downtown Miami and Orlando has height restrictions that are seriously enforced," said Joe. "Working for Adelia Earle has forced me to become far more familiar with building codes than I'd ever dreamed of. Every time we install a faucet at her place, it requires about fourteen town permits."

"Where's the golf course?" asked Bootsie. "This whole island looks smaller than your average golf club."

"It is a fact that the golf course mentioned in Chip's prospectus is bullshit," Gerda told her. "But this is interesting. I been researching all during ride down about this old hotel, and the HGTV star Sienna Blunt has listed on her design blog under 'Upcoming Projects' that she is working on this exact place. Also, she has a vacation cottage in Swan Island, which I discovered while Googling local real estate transactions."

"We need to get in touch with Sienna Blunt," said Joe. "The Colketts know her pretty well, and I hung out with her a little last January in Magnolia Beach." While Joe did some texting, we wandered around to see a large pool, currently empty of water, and a stretch of pretty beachfront.

"And look at this great old dock!" I said, admiring the weathered gray boards and a cute little skiff boat, herons and gulls flying around, and views of pristine water.

Then we both noticed a familiar-looking tanned, blond guy in a T-shirt and shorts casting a fishing rod about forty feet down the dock. An older man with dark hair was sitting next to him, talking on his cell phone.

"Is that Chip?" screamed Bootsie. "I'm going to kill him!"

THE OLDER MAN elbowed Chip, and the two jumped into a little outboard motorboat, sped away around the inlet, and disappeared.

"Chip is in *big* trouble! I'm texting Mummy right now!" said Bootsie. "She'll probably think I'm joking again, though," she realized, giving up.

"Maybe he's staying at the spinach place, too," offered Sophie. "We might run into him there! Because we only got twenty minutes to catch that ferry." Back in the minivan, we followed Google Maps, found the dock, unloaded the bags, and scrambled onto a beautifully maintained boat painted white and green for the three-minute ride to the hotel.

"I don't think Chip would stay at a vegan spa, even if he has been kidnapped," mused Bootsie.

"I got Sienna on the phone and invited her to meet us for drinks at Le Vert Epinard later," said Joe. "But Sienna burst into laughter and said there are no drinks at Le Vert, and to call her in the morning."

Joe kept talking on the quick boat ride as we passed gorgeous island homes and sped across the clearest water I've ever seen.

"According to Sienna's blog, she has a fabulous cottage right in Swan Island Village," he was saying, and was about to show us the pictures of said beach house, when suddenly a man dressed in all-white leaned down from the dock that the boat's captain was currently tying up to.

"Welcome to Le Vert Epinard! I'm Hans, the spa director. Please place your phones into this organic, nontoxic basket," he said. "Welcome to island bliss and complete immersion into a world where breathing, boot-camp-style workouts, and excessive perspiring of toxins is a way of life!"

Chapter Seventeen

"THEY CONFISCATED THE snacks, and the tequila, too," said Joe five minutes later, looking as upset as I've ever seen him. "You know that show *Naked and Afraid*? This is way worse."

Le Vert Epinard looked like something you'd see in *Town & Country*'s travel section, with gorgeous white cottages, tall palms, bougainvillea in bright purple bloom, and ocean views everywhere you looked.

While it was true that a margarita would have added to the joys of the island hotel, I was still thrilled to be in such a gorgeous spot, since it's not like pricey hotels are in my Progresso soup budget.

"It's just for a night," Holly told Joe. "I've been wanting to come to this place since it opened two years ago, but for some reason, Howard refused."

"I can't imagine why," grumbled Joe.

"Anyway, get over yourself! We're on the Total Deprivation Plan, which includes three hours of meditation on the beach interspersed with intensive interval workouts!" Holly said happily.

"They measure out the snacks of celery sticks and spinach leaves at 3 p.m. and 7 p.m., but there's unlimited lemon water all day."

"You're supposed to be getting the dirt on Scooter's partner Pete Penworthy!" screamed Joe. "How do beach meditation and leafy greens get you closer to finding Chip? And what about your future baby? It's going to need sustenance, and a nap!"

Holly gave Joe a concerned, pitying look, which made Joe angrier.

"I'm skipping the intense intervals because of my possible pregnancy, and Hans agreed I can have some organic rice crackers with my snack since I told him there's a seventeen percent chance I might have conceived on Thanksgiving night.

"Anyway, Mrs. Pete Penworthy said in the Miami newspaper story that Le Vert Epinard changed her life, and that her thighs are now as smooth as Rosie Huntington-Whitely's. She'll be here today," Holly told Joe, "and then I'll bond with her over a frond of chard and find out where Chip is."

"This is good plan," said Gerda approvingly. "I see on schedule it's time for me to attend Extreme Ab Explosion. Let's go."

"AMANDA PENWORTHY DIDN'T seem to know anything about Chip, but she did mention a cottage she and Pete own on Swan Key," Holly whispered to us two hours later as we all desperately sipped at lemon water. "She said her husband Pete and Scooter are there doing some fishing with a friend from Pennsylvania. And some business, but Amanda doesn't pay too much attention to anything Pete says."

"Chip!" screamed Bootsie into the balmy breeze to her absent brother, forgetting that we were supposed to be whispering. "He's definitely being held hostage at this secret fishing cottage. We're coming to save you!" she added, aiming this statement toward the mainland.

"Calm down," said Joe. "We need an exit strategy for Chip."

"My strategy is, we find Chip tomorrow, then beat the crap out of Scooter and Pete and take Chip with us," Bootsie told him.

"This could be dangerous," Gerda told her. "Scooter might look fancy with blue blazer and expensive shirts, but he has a gun and a Krampus mask, plus he could have scary friends."

"You know what we need?" said Sophie, motioning us toward a quiet grove of mangroves twenty feet from where Hans was looking suspiciously at us.

"We need to get the heck outta here!" finished Sophie. "Usually I'm all for a spa and I don't mind eating healthy, but we gotta get our phones back and rescue Chip. Then I need to get home, 'cause we got the town festival coming up, plus my cabaret was so awesome that I might want to do another one on New Year's Eve, which would take my mind off the fact that I was hoping to get married the next day, and I'm going to need a whole new song list and some new outfits."

"Good plan," said Joe, which was the first time he and Sophie had seen eye to eye in weeks. "Let's go."

"I asked one of the bellboys if there's a fun hotel nearby," Sophie added. "He gave me the 411 on a cool place called the Sugar Lime Inn which is right across the inlet. I paid the guy twenty dollars to use his phone and booked us six rooms at the Sugar Lime Inn, which has its own reggae band, a tiki bar, and a menu that includes everything this place doesn't! Think burgers, mahi-mahi tacos, and fried shrimp, clams, conch, and anything else that swims and can be breaded, fried, and dolloped with tartar sauce, lemon juice, and ketchup!"

Elation surged through me, and Joe and Bootsie's faces lit up. Le Vert Epinard was really nice, but not having my phone prevented me from checking on Waffles, and I don't have the stamina to make it through an interval workout session.

"Also, I paid the meditation therapist a hundred bucks to pick us up in her fishing boat in fifteen minutes," Sophie told us. "Because she said Hans is not happy when people leave early, and they tell you there are no more boats going to the mainland if you try to bolt.

"Gerda, you distract Hans, who's got the hots for ya, and Joe and Dave, you get the phones and the luggage."

"Where are the phones?" said Dave nervously. "Because I'm scared of Hans, who could definitely beat me up. And so could his wife, that co-spa director Martina, who's in better shape than Rhonda Rousey."

"That's true, and Hans and Martina are always lurking around the concierge hut where we checked in!" I agreed. "But on the plus side, Martina seems to have a thing for Joe. I noticed she told you that she liked your Lacoste workout shorts."

"Women love me." Joe shrugged. "What can I say? I keep getting better-looking every year. With the tan I've acquired spending so much time working for Mrs. Earle, I'm irresistible."

"Gerda and Joe could tell Hans and Martina to meet them in the Sweat Lodge," I suggested. "Just the name Sweat Lodge, sounds, well, you know." I made a vague gesture.

"They'll totally go for that," screamed Bootsie, who made a more specific gesture to indicate what Hans would be doing with

Gerda, given the opportunity—which, by the way, I didn't think was about to happen. I'm not sure Gerda believes in any kind of romantic exchanges, and she's definitely not one to engage in quickie make-out sessions.

"Dave, you be the messenger and set this all up. Then, you're going to move all the luggage down to the dock."

"Is there a worse word in the English language than 'sweat'?" pondered Joe. "It's so gross. Couldn't they call it the Perspiration Pavilion?"

"Sweat is sexy," Bootsie informed him. "That's why people go to gyms, and, I don't know, music festivals and food trucks and stadium concerts."

"None of which I go to," Joe told her.

"I'm on the luggage, but I don't want to be in charge of the phones," said Dave. "I could probably seduce someone!" he added hopefully. "Maybe Martina will like me, too."

"She is not interested in you, given that you are still in puberty," Gerda told him.

"Hurry up," Bootsie ordered Dave. "We're gonna need to make this getaway fast after you seize back the phones."

Holly sighed and agreed to leave, since she wasn't sure the rice crackers were going to be enough to quell her nausea.

"I feel kind of bad for Martina and Hans," I said. "It's really hot in the Sweat Lodge."

Bootsie fixed me with a stern eye.

"Kristin, do you or do you not want to get back to that dog of yours?" Bootsie said. " And do you or do you not want a frozen rum drink in approximately forty-five minutes, plus the use of your phone at an adorable, fun Florida Keys hotel with a gorgeous pool shaded by bougainvillea and that has a reggae band playing tonight at seven, and is offering every conceivable type of chilled seafood on ice in the Friday Night Raw Bar?"

"Um, I guess I want the frozen drink," I admitted.

"Dock in fifteen minutes!" said Sophie.

FOURTEEN MINUTES LATER, we were all at the dock, where the meditation teacher—who looked a lot less serene when she wasn't in her meditation caftan, and more like a regular Florida Keys gal in shorts and a tank top—was at the helm of a fishing boat. She welcomed us onto her boat with a cheery wave, and Gerda and Dave started piling the various items of baggage into the boat, with Dave assuring Holly he'd be extra careful with her stuff.

"Maybe I should stay till tomorrow," said Holly regretfully. "Because there's moonlight Tai Chi tonight and a special class on how to use turmeric in a facial that would give me the dewy skin of a Hadid sister."

"That can't be good for someone who's possibly pregnant," Joe informed her. "You need to eat, like, fried grouper or a turkey burger. Swiss chard isn't enough for someone in a delicate condition. Let's go. I got mildly groped by Martina, and I need alcohol."

"This spa was a wrong turn. We're supposed to be rescuing Chip!" Bootsie yelled at Holly.

"I, too, would like to stay here," Gerda said, "but better to focus on rescuing Chip."

"Sorry for the detour," said Holly, shrugging and reaching into the large basket of phones Dave had brought onto the boat. "I thought Amanda Penworthy would have all the answers. I'm sorry. Anyway, it's good to be all phoned up again. Maybe the Colketts found the barbecue person for the party, plus I need to check on the Trendy Tent's setup, too." With that, the meditation instructor started up her motor and neatly aimed her little fishing boat toward Swan Key.

"Hey, look at this gorgeous monogrammed iPhone cover!" said Sophie, who was rooting through the assemblage of phones next to Holly. "Is this, like Chanel?"

"Let me see that," said Bootsie. "The monogram says 'A.P.' Dave, you grabbed the wrong phone, but in this case, your fuckup has an upside. This is Amanda Penworthy's phone!" She immediately started punching at the phone and reading Mrs. Penworthy's texts and e-mails.

"This lady Amanda should have password-protected her device," Gerda observed.

"There's a text from Pete telling Amanda not to come to the place on Swan Key when she leaves Le Vert Epinard, but instead to go right to Miami!" Bootsie said. "He said some deals are going down in the Keys this weekend, and that Amanda would be real bored and should stay away." She looked up, eyes bulging angrily.

"The only thing going down in Swan Key is Pete Penworthy, who I'm going to, um, whack with a kayak paddle for kidnapping Chip!" she yelled into the wind as we buzzed across the little inlet. "And Scooter, if we can find his preppy ass!"

"I'll help," promised Dave. Then he paused, looking upset. "I forgot my new Brooks Brothers loafers at the spa!" screamed Dave, who was holding Holly's luggage on his lap, scrolling through his phone, and suddenly looked down at his feet, which were pale, scrawny, and encased in flip-flops bought that morning at the airport Ron Jon. "I loved those loafers."

"Dave, since you did a good job on the phones and the luggage, we're gonna get you new loafers," Sophie told him. "And I think we should let ya text your mom tonight just to check in. She must be real worried. As long as you don't tell her you were kidnapped, that is."

"I won't," Dave assured her. "In fact, I'm hoping it takes a few days to find Chip, because this is the greatest free vacation of my life!"

Chapter Eighteen

STEEL DRUM MUSIC was playing, palms were swaying, and the moon was shining across the water that evening at the Sugar Lime Inn, where we were sitting amid a happy crowd under a hibiscus-covered open-walled bar and restaurant. Ceiling fans spun slowly above, and thin-crust pizzas topped with lobster, burrata, and arugula were arriving at the table. Joe had vetoed a pie topped with baby spinach, telling the waiter that we'd just fled Le Vert Epinard, and that he would probably never feel the same about all vegetables in the leafy green family, and that even the arugula was pushing it.

We'd checked into adorable rooms, which were Caribbean-style with dark wood furniture, white bed linens, and excellent wi-fi and flat-screen TVs, and I'd checked on Waffles. Martha reported that she'd made him a gently sautéed chicken breast for dinner, and that Waffles was happily watching *Beverly Hills Chihuahua* nestled onto Martha's lap. I could relax! Waffles loves that movie.

Despite the fact that we hadn't yet figured out the details of the

Chip rescue operation, the Sugar Lime Inn had a distinctly festive air, and even Bootsie was in a good mood.

"This place is awesome!" said Sophie, sucking a frozen margarita through a straw. "That bellboy knew what he was talking about."

"Sienna Blunt's on her way over to meet us," said Joe, tossing aside his phone for the first time since we'd arrived. "As much as I think she's overrated, and I'm positive Sienna got her own show because she looks good in a tool belt, I'm going to become her new best friend if it'll help us wind up the hunt for Chip. I need to get out of the Keys and back to work ASAP, because Adelia's collection of vintage Florida-travel-themed coasters isn't going to organize itself.

"There's Sienna now. Hey, beautiful!" he called out to the TV personality, who did look fantastic in a little beige linen dress and flat sandals. "We escaped Shutter Island!"

After introductions and some commiserating about Le Vert Epinard, where Sienna had gone for a spa treatment once, then been lectured by Hans because she'd had a Snapple in her purse, we got down to business, and Sienna pulled an iPad out of her tote.

"It's weird that you called about L'Etoile Hotel, because I was so excited about the project when Pete Penworthy hired me to do some drawings for it last fall," she said. "That old place is adorable, and I have an amazing midcentury-modern-meets-South-Beach vision for it. Look at these renderings!" she said.

"Love the double-height yellow lacquered doors, the ten-foot ficus hedges, the lanterns, and the glass-tiled pool," Joe told her, admiring the images Sienna had produced.

"This looks nothing like my brother's prospectus!" observed Bootsie. "This is, like, a boutique hotel design."

"I'm totally getting this vibe," Joe told Sienna. "And, count me in if the job gets too big for one person. Florida sunny-chic-meets-golf-glamour is what I do best. I'm picturing blowing out that entrance even more, taking the front doors to a height of twenty feet, flanked by giant modern gold palm tree sculptures, and doormen handing out highball glasses filled with Arnold Palmers as you arrive, and misting stations in each outdoor space—"

"This project isn't happening!" yelled Bootsie. "Remember? The whole point is that investors like the Binghams were being sold on a huge property that could never fit on L'Etoile's current footprint. There's a thirty-five-foot height limit everywhere in the Keys. It's not going to be built!"

"I was told by Pete and a lawyer friend of his to sketch out the decor for a ten-room luxury hotel when we met in September, and that it would just be an extensive makeover of the existing building." Sienna shrugged. "Then, when I had a few ideas to show them, they said they'd gone in a different direction and changed their vision for the project, and that I should put my designs on hold. I heard a rumor that a big resort was coming to the area, but everyone in town told me that was impossible, because the zoning here is ironclad.

"Anyway," finished Sienna, "I only got one check. So I'm going back to my HGTV show, which is fun, but I've always dreamed of designing a hotel like this one, so if anything changes, let me know!"

"Was the lawyer you met a tanned, golf-playing type by the name of Scooter Simmons?" Bootsie asked Sienna.

"That was it!" confirmed Sienna. "He was a handsome guy, a real smooth talker."

"I'm guessing that Chip agreed to the boutique hotel plan, then got bamboozled into defrauding his friends," Holly said. "Anyway, the easiest way to spring Chip is to find Scooter, cozy up to him, and then have him lead us to Chip. Since I might be pregnant, Sophie should do it."

"I'll do it, but I'm not into it!" Sophie said. "Scooter is such a sneak. Penworthy sounds like he's just your basic scam artist, but, guess what, Sienna? Scooter's been dating this poor girl we know named Eula. He grabbed some gold she bought with her Powerball money, and he's also holding up Chip for fifty grand, too!"

A tanned, blond woman somewhere in her early forties, wearing a crisp silk sheath dress, turned around from her seat at the next table to face us.

"Excuse me," she said. "You aren't talking about Scooter Simmons of Magnolia Beach, are you? Because I met Scooter on the *Palace of the Seas* last month," she added, sipping her drink and crossing her legs. "And I'm his fiancée."

OVER MORE DRINKS, our new acquaintance, whose name was Minnie Allington, told us how Scooter had met her during a ping-pong tournament the third day of the cruise. He'd been so attentive over the ensuing three months that they'd actually gotten engaged just a week ago, before Scooter had left for a meeting in Pennsylvania. Since Minnie had overheard most of our conversation of the last hour, she now realized that Scooter's "business trip" was part Eula, part phony hotel deal, and one-hundred-percent shady.

"How'd he date you and Eula on the same boat?" marveled Sophie. "Didn't ya know he had another girlfriend?"

"The boat is fairly large," Minnie said, taking a drag on a Marlboro Silver. "I mean, there's the movie theater, the poker and mah-jongg lounge, three different bars, a disco, the gym, and the spa. Naturally, there's a pool, a Starbucks, and a jogging path, plus there's the basketball court."

"How much is this cruise again?" asked Sophie, looking interested.

"You don't want to know. Anyway, when I give it some thought, Scooter did start getting a little cagey about where he was a lot of the time," said Minnie reflectively. "He started going to daily art classes, and then he told me he was plein-air painting every afternoon," Minnie said. "And one or two nights a week, he'd say he was having a quiet dinner in his suite so he could catch up on new episodes of *The Walking Dead*."

"He was catching up on Eula!" Sophie told her. "Sorry," she added. "If it makes you feel any better, Minnie, Eula told us she and Scooter never got naked together. So Scooter technically didn't cheat on you, although he did indicate he was gonna propose to Eula on New Year's Eve. But you know Scooter's always trying to find easy money, and she's real rich."

"So am I," Minnie told her, waving down the bartender for another drink. "But from what you're telling me about this Powerball girl, Scooter must have figured out that she was a better revenue stream than I am."

"The only way to reach Scooter's cold golf ball of a heart is money," Joe told Minnie. "I'm sure he liked you better, though, since Eula is an absolute nightmare, despite her new blond highlights. Maybe that's why Scooter grabbed all that gold from Eula, so he can come down here and marry you."

"This one might have made out with Eula!" Sophie told Minnie, pointing at Joe. "Which is real hypocritical. But you know, love and hate are supposedly based on the same chemical in the brain.

Or something. Anyway, sorry you got engaged to such a jerk. I married one myself."

"The only thing I'm interested in engaging with Scooter on at this point is revenge," Minnie informed us. "I'm going to help you rescue your brother," she added to Bootsie, "and in the process, I'll happily screw over Scooter. Who, in a lucky twist of fate, I'm scheduled to meet right here for lunch tomorrow afternoon."

MINNIE EXCUSED HERSELF to go puff on her cigarette on a beach lounge chair and do some thinking, then returned to the table with a little smile on her elegant face.

"You need a fake investor," observed Minnie, stabbing an olive in her drink with a tiny skewer and popping it into her mouth. "Someone who Scooter thinks has big money. Then the phony moneybags gets a meeting with Scooter and Pete. Also, we ask them to bring Chip along to the fake meeting. I can arrange everything for tomorrow at lunchtime," Minnie told us.

"How will that work?" Bootsie asked, intrigued. "And can I wear a disguise? Because I'm excellent at portraying myself as a postal clerk, a hotel housekeeper, or really anyone in uniform. The Coast Guard springs to mind right now, given our seaside setting."

"I think it's better if the fake investor is temperamental, takes a sudden and irrational dislike to Chip, and has him banished from the meeting, and from being involved in any way in the deal," Minnie told her. "Then you can just hit the road with your brother. And I like where you're going with wearing a borrowed or stolen official outfit of some kind, but that won't help us with pretending to have a moneybags friend interested in L'Etoile and other deals with Scooter and Pete."

"That actually makes a lot of sense," Bootsie said. "We somehow convince Scooter and Pete Penworthy that Chip's a liability. Which he is," she added. "Chip's too honest to roll out a resort scam."

"We can't pose as investors, though, Minnie. The only one of us who Scooter won't recognize is Gerda," said Holly. "He's seen Gerda plenty of times, actually, but Gerda tends to blend in due to her fondness for black Nike tracksuits. No offense, Gerda."

"None taken," said Gerda. "I do not like to be flashy."

"Uh-huh," said Minnie, assessing the Pilates pro, who was currently listening and also lecturing one of the waiters about how she wanted an alcohol-free smoothie with fresh ginger, coconut, beet tops, and there had better not be any added sugar in it, even though the name of the hotel included that dangerous substance.

"You know what? That girl who wants the smoothie looks a little like someone I know in Miami. She's in the restaurant business, and she invests in small hotels," Minnie told us. "We can get Gerda to pose as my friend Brunhilda Dagmar!"

"That sounds awesome!" said Sophie. "Does she look like Gerda?"

"Brunhilda is tall, European, stern, and dressed to the nines," Minnie told her, whipping out her phone. "Here's a pic from the Miami Restaurant Association Dinner, which is a more relaxed look for her."

She showed us a snapshot of an unsmiling, perfectly made-up woman with swoopy blond waves and a severe blue sheath dress with silk scarf, pearls, pricey Chanel pumps, and a matching handbag.

"That's relaxed?" said Sophie dubiously.

The picture of Brunhilda called to mind Martha Stewart mixed with Ursula Andress. We all swiveled from the photo to Gerda, and Minnie's idea sort of started to make sense.

In her current look, which was workout clothes and sans a drop of makeup, Gerda didn't evoke expensive-European-restaurant-owner vibes, and Gerda was probably ten years younger than Brunhilda. But there *was* a resemblance.

"I myself will admit that this woman Brunhilda could be my older sister," offered Gerda. "Although I think she spend too much on needless luxury items, which I would never do. Money is better spent on investments and on equipment such as skis, tennis rackets, and Pilates reformer machines."

"The more I think about it, it's better if we convince Scooter to leave the U.S. for a while. I'd like to make sure he's not back on the *Palace of the Seas* next month. Let's tell him there's money to be made somewhere really far away. Like, a twelve-hour flight away," mused Minnie.

"What about Siberia?" said Sophie. "I've always heard it's real cold there, and Scooter would freeze his nuts off!"

"That could be good," agreed Bootsie. "I'd love to send Scooter to Siberia."

"What's in Siberia, anyway?" asked Holly.

Joe did some Googling, and showed us photos of majestic mountains with snowy alpine vistas.

"Looks pretty nice," Bootsie said, disappointed. "Who knew Siberia was so beautiful? It could be the next pick for *Condé Nast Traveler*'s Hot List, and with our luck, Scooter might think he's on a swanky ski vacation. I mean, obviously it looks cold, so if he got pushed into a snowdrift and fell off a mountain that would be good, but I'm not sure how we'd arrange that from a beach bar in Florida."

"This gives me good idea," said Gerda. "I can get my cousins to meet Scooter in Austria, lured there by fake business deal, and then scare him a little. Not to beat the crap out of him, but maybe follow him around the town and freak him out. He could maybe get locked overnight in a mountain cabin." At this Gerda smiled, which she rarely does.

"I'm liking it," Minnie Allington said, clapping her hands and doing a little hair flip. "I'll pay for the one-way ticket to Zurich! The fake Brunhilda is going to get Scooter to think there's an amazing business opportunity in the Austrian Alps," Minnie told her. "Gerda, you'll need to lose the black Nike tracksuit to play Brunhilda. Also, you need professional hair, makeup and a push-up bra. And a tasteful sheath dress."

"I'm excellent at shopping," Sophie assured her. "Where's the nearest place to get some fancy clothes for Gerda?"

"I think the Off Fifth Saks Outlet in the Dolphin Mall near Miami is the way to go," Minnie said. "If you can get hair, makeup, and the outfit done and be back here for lunch by 1:15 tomorrow afternoon, we have a plan."

"I'm on it!" Sophie shrieked. "This is gonna be awesome!"

Chapter Nineteen

AT 8:30 A.M., all of us except Joe, Bootsie, and Dave piled into the minivan and headed north to the Dolphin Mall. The first stop was a salon called the Blow Bar, where we dropped Gerda, with Holly there for moral support, since Gerda was muttering darkly about strangers touching her and how she did not enjoy having her hair blown out and that hair spray is full of toxic chemicals.

Meanwhile, Sophie, Minnie Allington, and I went right to a rack of dresses in the Saks Off Fifth store.

"Who's Brunhilda's favorite designer? Escada? Max Mara? Michael Kors?" breathed Sophie excitedly. "Akris? Oscar? Diane von Furstenberg? I want Gerda to look amazing! I mean, I've been trying to get her out of a tracksuit for the last three years! One time last summer I got her into a jumpsuit, but that's not all that different from her usual look."

"Let's go with the St. John sheath dress in pink with the notched neckline, princess seams, a two-inch front slit for easy movement. It's a classic Florida look," Minnie said, removing this garment from the rack, "and we'll top it off with a floral silk scarf. Does your friend have Spanx?"

"I don't think Gerda needs Spanx," I told Minnie. "She's one-hundred-percent muscle."

"Ya think she's a four or a six?" wondered Sophie, examining the tags on the pink dresses. "Who can tell under that tracksuit?"

"Get the four," advised Minnie. "Brunhilda likes things very fitted, which is flattering on a tall girl. Now, I have my salesperson from Chanel meeting us in the parking lot in five minutes, since we don't have time to make a run to the boutique."

"Darn it!" screamed Sophie. "A Chanel store would really cheer me up. But I guess buying the bag and shoes in a parking lot is better than nothing. What did ya get her?"

"The large messenger bag with the shoulder strap, chain details, and gold double-C clasp," Minnie told her. "Sporty, yet expensive. And a classic cap-toe pump."

On the ride back south after we picked up a fabulously coiffed Gerda and Holly, Minnie told us she'd done some late-night texting with Scooter, and had mentioned to him that her wealthy friend Brunhilda Dagmar might be stopping by at lunch today, too, and she hoped it would be okay, and that she'd added that Dagmar was also looking for a new lawyer to work with her on a planned new super-spa over in Austria. Maybe it could be Scooter, Minnie had hinted, and he'd readily agreed.

IT WAS ALREADY 1 p.m. by the time we got back to the Sugar Lime, where we zipped a reluctant Gerda into the pink dress, inserted her into the fancy shoes, and stuck the messenger bag over her arm.

"Sunglasses," said Holly, placing a large pair on Gerda's nose.

"Now, you know what to do, Gerda, right? I mean, Brunhilda. First, you interest Scooter in a fake ski resort."

"And don't forget to convince Scooter and Pete that the deal hinges on Chip being out of the picture," Sophie said. "I got my lawyer to e-mail me a release for Chip from the L'Etoile deal, and I just printed it out for ya." She stuck a document in the messenger bag.

"We just have to hope Chip either doesn't recognize Gerda, or figures out that she's trying to rescue him," Joe added. "Chip's not the smartest guy around, but I think he'll realize something's up and keep quiet."

"I am ready." Gerda nodded.

"I'm calling your phone right now, Gerda," said Sophie. "Answer it, and leave it on. That way we can stay out of sight but hear the whole lunch. And, we can bust in and help you and Chip if ya need us."

Gerda nodded and marched gingerly in her fancy heels to the patio, where we could see Minnie seated at a prime table with the three men. The rest of us lurked on Sophie's private patio, which was to the right of the restaurant, and screened by some lush tropical foliage.

"Chip!" screamed Bootsie, sotto voce, staring through the bougainvillea fronds at her brother. "He looks terrible!"

"Not really," said Joe. "I mean, he has a tan, he looks like he's been working out, and he just ordered a beer. It's not that bad to be kidnapped down in the Keys."

"That's true," said Dave. "I've really enjoyed it myself."

"Hello, Minnie Allington," we heard Gerda's muffled voice say via Sophie's phone. "It is I, your friend Brunhilda Dagmar, the wealthy restaurateur and investor. What a pleasure to join you here at lunch."

"Gerda's a horrible actress," said Bootsie. "We should have rehearsed her more."

"I think Chip just realized it's Gerda!" offered Sophie. "Looks like he choked on his guacamole. But he's staying quiet."

"They're buying it," Joe said. "Scooter just pulled up a chair for Brunhilda. I mean, for Gerda."

OVER LUNCH, SCOOTER and Pete told the fake Brunhilda all about their plans for L'Etoile, which would be an amazing resort and the first in all of the Keys to get special permission to build a glitzy high-rise. Gerda-as-Brunhilda said she'd give them a check as soon as she got to a bank, because she wanted in on the deal.

Then Minnie gave the men her spiel about an Austrian ski retreat she and Brunhilda were planning, which would offer shares to the right investors, and that Brunhilda needed a top American legal brain for the ski project, for which this lawyer would be paid twenty-five thousand dollars per month. Gerda-as-Brunhilda agreed that Scooter was the man for the job. Then she turned her sunglasses toward Chip.

"This person cannot be involved in my restaurant and boutique hotel," said Gerda, voice crackling through her handbag and out of Sophie's phone. "He is too American for my vision of Austrian resort, which has no place for a man in a T-shirt. Pete and Scooter, if you remove this tall blond man from my presence, we can proceed with our deal."

"Sure!" said Pete. "Chip, hit the road."

"Also, this young man looks like type who screw up a lot," continued Gerda in frosty, judgmental tone (which wasn't all that much of an acting job for her). It did, though, sound like she was warming up to her role as international tycooness. "I need clean slate if we going to launch fabulous projects together," Gerda told Scooter. "So if this person Chip owes you money, I want you to forget his debt right now. And, sign a legal document to that effect, filling in his name here, and your name, here."

"Really?" said Pete dubiously. "Um, okay, but this guy was fifty grand in the hole with us."

"This is what I'm talking about," said Gerda. "Small-time thinking is not what Brunhilda Dagmar is all about. Deal is off if you don't sign."

"Okay, okay," said Pete hastily, and we saw him scribble his name on the paper.

Just then, a big black limo pulled up to the restaurant entrance. Two huge guys got out of the back, looked around, saw Pete and Scooter, nodded, and started heading over to their table.

"Mayday! Mayday!" screamed Bootsie into her phone, which, set on mute and buried inside Gerda's blingy new Chanel purse, was doing nothing to warn her. "Gerda, some actual scary people have just arrived!"

Chapter Twenty

WE ALL RUSHED out from our hiding spot and onto the restaurant's patio. Chip gave Bootsie a huge hug, seemingly unconcerned that two thugs were now looming over his table.

Things devolved quickly. Minnie informed Scooter that not only was their engagement off, but that she might report him for fraud, since apparently he'd been selling fake hotel shares to unsuspecting older folks in Pennsylvania.

"What's all this?" said one of the guys from the limo. "Pete, we came to tell you that your boss in Miami has been waiting for some cash from this L'Etoile deal, and if you're skimming all the money for yourself, which it sounds like you are, you might want to jump in the ocean and start swimming."

"Just so you know, my brother here was scammed, too!" Bootsie told the guys. "He really thought this was a boutique hotel deal until a couple of weeks ago. Then he didn't know how to get out of it, and was told he owed these guys fifty thousand dollars."

"Listen, lady, our beef is mostly with Pete," said the guys. "Your brother isn't worth our time and effort. Pete here made the mistake of screwing over our boss on this hotel deal, and he's not happy."

The guys explained that their boss, one Theodore Martin from Miami Shores, Florida, had long owned the L'Etoile property, and had asked Pete to look into developing it. Then Mr. Martin started to hear around town that Pete Penworthy was lying to people and taking deposits for a much bigger hotel deal. "He's going to shut down the fake hotel deal," said the shorter of the two guys from Miami.

"I'm completely innocent!" Scooter told them, jumping up. "So I'm just going to skedaddle. And if I can ever be of any help, or provide introductions to any people in Magnolia Beach—"

"Shut it and sit down," said the bigger guy. Scooter sat again.

"What about this guy?" asked his colleague, indicating Chip. "Who are you?"

"Chip Delaney!" said Chip. "Golf equipment salesman. I was hoping to get into the hotel game, but I guess it's not going to work out."

"Beat it," the guy told him. "I can't be bothered with you."

"We are about to leave," said Gerda, "but can you guarantee us that no one gonna pursue Chip here anymore and leave him threatening notes? Because he don't have a lot of money, and he's not a wheeler-dealer type."

The smaller guy eyed Gerda, and appeared to like what he saw. "Sure, honey, and who are you?" he asked. "I like your style. Tall and tan and European. And the Chanel shoes. Very nice."

"Sorry," Gerda told him, "I'm focused on my career and I don't have time to date."

Just then, a party van pulled up behind the limo, and the entire restaurant turned to stare as a dozen ladies in their seventies, clad in caftans and Lilly Pulitzer dresses and large sunglasses, emerged. One petite, smiling lady was waving in our direction, and she looked very familiar.

"Is that . . . Adelia Earle?" I asked Joe, who looked panicked and nodded.

"That's her, and her Friday afternoon bridge club," he confirmed. "She called me about her antique coasters last night, and I'd had a lot to drink, and she somehow got it out of me that we were all at the Sugar Lime Inn and just a two-hour drive from Magnolia Beach!"

"Hi, Mrs. Earle," said Gerda, who'd met the tobacco heiress with us last winter, and had always liked her. "How are you? How are all your friends that you have lunch with each day? I enjoy seeing you again."

"The girls are doing great!" said Adelia, indicating the group of women, who were headed to the bar. "We all love Joe, and it was the perfect excuse to ride down here for lunch."

Adelia caught sight of Scooter and shook her finger at him. "You naughty boy, Scooter, are you in trouble again?"

"Not at all," said Scooter nervously. "I'm, uh, just here visiting friends. Reading, boating, jogging, that's it!"

"Scooter and this guy Pete have gotten my brother into a major shit storm, Mrs. E.," Bootsie told the caftan-clad heiress. "They involved him in an investment scam on an old hotel called L'Etoile, which was supposed to become a super-fancy resort with one hundred condos, two restaurants, a spa, and a disco, but is only zoned for about twelve rooms. And these two guys have a boss who actually owns the property, and isn't too happy."

"I know L'Etoile!" said Mrs. Earle, her small face taking on a nostalgic glow behind her large sunglasses. "That was a favorite spot of mine and my late husband. We used to go there every New Year's Eve. It was so romantic. We'd play tennis, swim, go fishing, and dance under the stars."

"The owner, Mr. Martin, said he doesn't have time to renovate the place," said the taller Miami guy to Mrs. Earle. "I'm real sorry, because I can see from how much you liked it that it must have been a special spot back in the day. But he has a bunch of projects in Miami right now, and he can't be coming down to the Keys all the time to supervise the place."

Just then, the guy caught sight of a tall redhead entering the restaurant, heading for the bar.

"Hey, there's Sienna Blunt from HGTV!" said the thug excitedly. "I love her! Wow, what a celebrity!"

"Hi, Sienna," said Joe without much enthusiasm. "What, is this the only restaurant in town? Does everyone eat lunch here?"

"It actually is the only place in town!" Sienna told him cheerfully. "Oh, there's the investor I'm meeting, who's down here on a fishing trip. Maybe you know her. She's one of the biggest restaurateurs in Miami!"

"That blond lady?" asked Gerda. "In a pink dress? Wait—she looks just like me."

"Uh-oh," said Bootsie. "I think the actual Brunhilda Dagmar is here."

Chapter Twenty-one

TWENTY MINUTES LATER, with explanations given all around, Sienna Blunt was showing Mrs. Earle and the real Brunhilda her designs for the old L'Etoile Hotel.

"I designed an updated look for the old building, and a spa, and a cool indoor-outdoor restaurant," Sienna explained. "Think of the best of the 1940s South Beach hotels mingled with California midcentury modern and classic preppy Palm Beach. Lots of white marble with bright yellow accents, and gardens full of bougainvillea and lemon trees."

Sienna scrolled through her iPad.

"The scale, of course, needs to be low, lush, and loungey," she was saying, "while staying leafy and beachy."

"Anyone knows that!" snorted Joe. "I mean, it's the Keys, not Las Vegas."

"Have you ever thought of having a clay pigeon shooting range there?" asked Adelia. "And doing the restaurant all in Lilly Pulitzer prints?"

She turned to the scary Miami guys. "I have a group of friends over there at the bar who are always looking for fun weekend getaways, and I'm thinking L'Etoile could make a glamorous comeback. Brunhilda might invest, and my bridge club has money, and, of course, my family are the Stokes cigarette people. So if your boss is willing to sell, this girl and I could bring back L'Etoile's glory days!"

"Sure, he's real interested in unloading the place," the taller guy told her. "I'll text him and run this past him. I mean, it's a shame to let it just sit there, and your ideas sound real nice."

"Mrs. Earle, you should know that there is other spa nearby that will be competition for your L'Etoile idea," Gerda told her, making her usual effort to quash any good mood that happened to be in her presence. "It's called Le Vert Epinard, and is very well-known among movie stars, with all food grown organically on site."

"I've been there, dear, and it was pure hell," Adelia told her. "L'Etoile is going to be fun, with the best margaritas for miles. Think of a spa that serves tequila, bacon, cheese, and pasta."

"Sienna will need help on a job this size!" said Joe hopefully to Mrs. Earle. "And I'm almost done with the renovation of your run-down shack—I mean that adorable cottage—and I'm available!"

"Our boss says he's good with selling to these two ladies and to send him the paperwork," said the taller Miami guy, reading a text message. "So we're done here, and we're taking Pete with us," he said, nudging Pete out of his chair. "What about this guy?" he said, indicating Scooter.

"We have a plan for him ourselves," Minnie told the muscular guys. "He was engaged to me and about to propose to another girl at the same time."

"That stinks," the bigger guy told Scooter. "You should be ashamed of yourself."

"Scooter, your stepmother Susie isn't going to like this!" Adelia added.

"I really need to get going," Scooter said. "I have a flight to Austria to catch. I'm all packed and ready to go, and I left my bags at the concierge desk. I think things have worked out really well here! Give my love to Eula," he said.

With that, Scooter made a beeline to the concierge, who handed over the blue Samsonite. Gerda and Joe grabbed it from him, with the Miami guys looking on as we explained that the bag had been stolen from the same girl Scooter had misled in Philly.

Scooter took one look at the huge guys' disapproving faces, gave up on the Samsonite, and headed toward the hotel exit toting only an expensive-looking briefcase. He was hustling off the shady terrace of the Sugar Lime Inn when, unfortunately, in his haste, the briefcase got caught on a branch of a potted orange tree, the lock popped, and the briefcase fell open.

Diamond necklaces and bracelets tumbled out onto the wood floor of the outdoor restaurant, and the happy din of diners enjoying conch-salad lunches ground to a halt.

"Eula's jewelry!" shrieked Sophie. "And wait a minute, that's my Gucci watch! I've been looking for that since it disappeared the other night at the country club. Scooter musta grabbed it right off my wrist."

"And there are my Tiffany drop earrings and my Cartier diamond necklace, which I thought I lost on the *Palace of the Seas*," said Minnie.

"And all the antique jewelry stolen from the Lemieuxs," said Holly. "We'll just take that with us, because December's almost over, and my shopping embargo is going to be done in less than ten days!"

Chapter Twenty-two

WE FLEW HOME that afternoon, dropped off the Samsonite to Eula—minus two gold bars, since Gerda had decided that keeping four was too many and not nice, while Joe said that it had been a real pain in the ass to go all the way to Florida, and one wasn't enough. We gave Eula a short explanation that Scooter would be in Europe for a while, and that we hoped she would find a much better guy to date very soon—maybe even on the *Palace of the Seas*.

I picked up Waffles at Holly's house, and enjoyed a blissful sleep and an uneventful Monday morning the next day at The Striped Awning. Outside on the town square, Sophie and Gerda were bossing around volunteers for the town festival decorating committee, and I snapped a few pictures of the decorations and texted them to John in California. Now that I was back from Florida, my missing-boyfriend malaise had returned. Maybe I'd simply call John and plead with him to come back for Christmas. Or I could try to guilt him into returning! Of course, Sophie had tried similar tactics with Joe vis-à-vis their engagement, and look how that had turned out.

Meanwhile, Eddie from the Pub showed up and reorganized a large table and some chairs in the back of my shop for his first poker game, which was set for 10 p.m. the next night. Holly was home with the Colketts, who had found the barbecue guy in Delaware, and were currently decorating the heated Trendy Tent party space.

At six, Joe stopped in and hit the Maker's Mark, throwing a tiny candy cane into his drink as a garnish.

"Adelia's been calling me all day. Her ideas sound fantastic for L'Etoile," Joe said glumly. "She'll probably make another gazillion dollars to add on to her current tobacco fortune. Her friends alone will book up all the rooms." He gave a glum wave as Sophie, Gerda, Bootsie, and Holly walked in.

"Anyway, Adelia's not sure that Sienna's going to need any help with L'Etoile, so she's keeping me on coasters and napkins for now."

"You know what?" Sophie said, plopping down in a chair and propping up her tiny boots on a footstool. "I think we need to take a break. Can't we do something fun, like order in food and watch holiday movies on the giant screen in Holly's new Man Shed, and she can show us where that moonshine thingy was supposed to go?"

"What kind of food?" said Bootsie. "And I'm in, whatever kind of food it is, but can it be something with meat and cheese?"

"Will there be gluten? Because I don't approve, if so," intoned Gerda.

"There's gonna be gluten," Bootsie told her. "And beer. I got the Hoagie House menu right here," and she whipped out a colorful tri-fold.

"You know what I've always wondered—mostly when I'm real bored, like when I'm getting my highlights touched up, or waiting for the Colketts to look through about four thousand paint colors—what's the difference between a grinder and a hoagie?" pondered Sophie, looking over the menu. "I mean, I mostly eat salads and stuff like that since I'm only four-eleven, and I gotta stay lean, but I like to eat junk food sometimes, and I feel like I should know."

"I think grinders have a toasted roll," Bootsie told her.

"Grinders are, like, hot, gooey chicken parmesan, and grinders always have cheese," said Joe, with some authority. "Hoagies are cold, like turkey or salami."

"You're all wrong," said Jared, who'd just parked his Uber Yukon to pick up Gerda. "I worked for Mike's Pizza two summers ago and there's no difference. It's just that people who have, like, PMS, or are home alone late at night like the word 'grinder.'"

"Huh," said Gerda. "Sounds porny. Is it sexual?"

"I like to keep food and sex separate!" shrieked Sophie. "Trust me, it's gross when someone's eating in bed. And I should know!"

"I AM STARTING to feel guilty about the extra gold brick," Gerda told us over the sandwiches which we were eating at Holly's house. "Tomorrow, I'm gonna go with Sophie to return the extra one to Eula. Even though she not so nice. Joe, you gonna have to deal with it."

"Eula won Powerball thanks to us!" shouted Bootsie. "She should be sending us all, like, champagne and Godiva chocolates from that crazy ship she's thankfully about to get back on. I feel entitled to a shipment of antique silver trays and diamond bracelets from wherever the next stop is via the *Palace of the Seas*. The gold is totally within our rights."

"I'm shocked to hear myself saying this, because normally I'd love to grab Eula's undeclared gold from the Caribbean, but I've come around. Let's just keep the one bar, sell it, and split the proceeds," offered Joe. "I'm too tired to tangle with Eula. If she says one Eula-ish thing, I'll be tempted to remind her that I've known her since before she had a glowy tan and Lanvin boots. I don't want to have to use the words 'low-heeled pumps,' but I might bust those out if I get really angry."

"I am looking forward to the New Year with new gym location," said Gerda. "And we still get the nine thousand, seven hundred fifty dollars. Plus, I then pay back Holly and Sophie for pricey Chanel handbag."

Gerda looked down at the gorgeous Chanel messenger bag with evident pride. "That purse really jazzes up your tracksuit, Gerda," Sophie told her. "You don't owe us a thing. It makes a perfect Christmas present for ya!"

"You should use the gold brick money to put a down payment on a house," suggested Holly, who had actually eaten part of a chicken parmesan grinder. "I know you love Eula's place and were thinking of making an offer.

"And, it works out perfectly, because I have a new and improved two-part plan to permanently evict Eula from this town," Holly added happily, "and Gerda, you buying her house is step one!"

"Okay, I make offer in the morning when we bring over the gold," agreed Gerda happily, gathering up the Chanel bag.

"What's the second part of this Eula plan?" asked Joe. "Because we already won her the Powerball, and she's still here."

"Don't worry," Holly told him, calming down slightly as she looked at an incoming text on her phone. "By tomorrow night, after the town festival and during my Christmas party, I will have Eula ready to scamper back to that boat as fast as her tiny and annoying feet can take her."

At that moment, the Colketts walked in from the party tent, looking upbeat, slightly tipsy, and completely spotless and unwrinkled despite twelve hours of party setup. Behind them was a good-looking guy in his forties with brown hair, nice blue eyes, wearing jeans and a parka, who brought with him a delicious scent of what could only be brisket that had been dry-rubbed and smoked for seven to ten hours.

"Meet our new best friend, Billy the Barbecue Master," said Tim. "He's got his mobile smoker truck on-site, Holly, and he's better than we remembered!"

Just then, Bootsie's phone dinged. "It's Officer Walt," she said. "He says there's been an explosion in Eula's toolshed."

Chapter Twenty-three

"THAT TRIP TO Florida gave me a lot of perspective," Sophie told me the next day at The Striped Awning, giving Waffles a small pat on the head while sipping a giant latte. For her part, Gerda helped me dust a top shelf I couldn't reach.

"First of all, I can't believe that missing moonshine boiler thingy was in Eula's shed! And do ya believe her when she says she didn't steal it, and didn't know it was in there?" Sophie asked me.

"I think she's telling the truth," I said. "I mean, Eula's getting back on the boat in a few days,. And she could buy her own booze equipment if she wanted to, plus I can't see her setting up a stolen still."

"Huh, I wonder how that thing got over to Eula's place. Anyway, Kristin, I had an awesome idea," Sophie told me. "I know your store makes, like, almost zero cash, so the Colketts and I are gonna bring the cabaret to The Striped Awning! For one night only, live at The Striped Awning, coming in January!"

I tried to picture how this would work. Where would they set up the upright bass, and how would Sophie do her dance moves in such a small space?

Since I'm no position to argue with any idea that might bring in even a single new customer, I thanked her profusely.

"And no matter what happens with Joe, I'm going to finish up my divorce. Like, pronto," Sophie added. "I'm willing to give Barclay any of my shoes except the Giuseppe Zanottis, and I'll return his collection of restaurant menus from the Umbria and Tuscany regions that he scrapbooked during our marriage.

"There's an all-new Sophie Shields happening in the new year, and she's going to be a fabulous divorcée!"

"I might be single again myself," I admitted. "I haven't gotten a call or text from John in the last forty-eight hours, and it's almost Christmas. I'm starting to realize that the holidays might be a great time to fall in love for some people, but they're also prime time for breakups."

"I, too, have gained some wisdom while on our trip over the weekend," announced Gerda. "Though I don't approve of Brunhilda, the restaurateur who I impersonated, I find myself inspired by a certain adventurous quality this lady has, as well as the resilience of Minnie Allington. These ladies make me want to possibly expand Bust Your Ass Gym even more. Possibly, I get a YouTube channel and maybe an app."

Chapter Twenty-four

"THANK GOODNESS THE holidays will be over soon," said Gerda that night as we parked in Holly's crowded driveway. "There is too much alcohol served this time of year."

"This is awesome!" I said, admiring the tent as we walked into the heated enclosure over Holly's backyard. Red roses were in huge, full, low arrangements on rustic wooden tables, and more roses were hanging in massive planters from the ceiling in gorgeous profusion. A temporary dance floor had been set up over the patio, and a Prince cover band was warming up on a stage as we took in a massive bar topped with a canopy of spruce branches, pinecones, and more red roses.

"Hey, there. Is John the vet back?" asked Mike Woodford, who was standing at the bar, where guys in Billy's Barbecue T-shirts were serving glasses of potent eggnog.

"Not yet," I told him. "But at least I can spend New Year's Eve with Waffles."

"I'll take you to dinner on New Year's Eve," offered Mike. "I can't promise you we'll sit at Table 11, but I know we could have a nice meal and be back before midnight for Waffles."

"Great offer," said a familiar voice from somewhere above my left ear. "But I'm home, and I'm going to take Kristin to dinner on New Year's Eve. At least I hope so."

John was back! Looking tall, handsome, steady, and spectacular in a navy blazer and jeans!

While I hugged John and absorbed his surprise return, Mike shrugged and left to go talk to Howard, and Bootsie handed John and me glasses of eggnog.

"This Christmas is going to be amazing! And so is this party," I said, looking around the candlelit tent. "Mason jar drinks, rustic burlap napkins, paper cones full of French fries and Tater Tots, and cornbread!"

"This is fantastic!" Bootsie seconded.

"Please don't ever mention Tater Tots again," Holly told me. "But I agree that the Colketts did an amazing job for a twenty-seven-hour party prep."

"There's no barbecue place that looks this fancy, but that's okay!" said Bootsie. "Because they just brought out the brisket sliders on potato rolls. Let me at them!"

"Look at Howard," said Holly with a sigh. "He looks so happy chomping on that sandwich."

"I haven't seen him smile like that since he bought that truck company in Indianapolis," observed Joe. "Maybe we should expand the poor guy's man cave and install a bar, a pool table, and a sports screening room. As much as all of those thoughts horrify me," he added.

As Abby, Ronnie, and Skipper from the country club started dancing to "*Little Red Corvette*," Eula walked in.

"Hi Eula," said Holly airily. "I'm glad Officer Walt freed you on your own recognizance after you convinced him you didn't steal the moonshine still from Howard's Man Shed. Luckily, I've already ordered another one, since the one you took exploded."

"I didn't take it, which Walt knows!" Eula said angrily. "And obviously, I can afford my own still, if I ever wanted one, which I don't! Someone framed me. Probably you," she said to Joe.

"If I'd only thought of it, I would have," he told her.

"Um, Holly," said Jared, popping up at her side in a red holiday sweater. "I have something I need to tell you, and I feel real guilty about it. I, um, stole your home distillery last week. I think I'm in love with you, and I get real jealous thinking about your husband. So I used my fake ID to buy a six-pack one night last week, got super-drunk, and then loaded up the still into the Yukon!

"When I woke up at six the next morning, the only place I could think of to put it was in Eula's shed, 'cause she lives right next door to me. Sorry it took down your shed when it blew up," he told Eula.

"No harm done," Holly told Jared. " If you can assemble the new still I bought this week and make sure it doesn't explode, that would be fabulous. I'll pay you overtime, too."

Chapter Twenty-five

"Is that Nick from Dunkin' Donuts as Prince?" I asked, impressed, after Eula had stormed off to the bar, and Holly had promised Jared she wouldn't tell Walt about the still.

"Absolutely," said Holly. "Nick does an amazing rendition of *Purple Rain*. You're going to love it."

"Did Prince do holiday songs?" asked Bootsie. "Because nothing comes to mind."

Just then, the band broke into "1999."

"Huh," Bootsie amended. "I guess this counts. I mean, usually this song comes at the end of, say, a New Year's Eve party, but then again, it works to kick off a festive night."

"These guys also do a lot of Flo Rida and Pitbull," the Colketts told us. "So get ready to bust a move!"

"Is that *Dave* in the Prince band?" exploded Bootsie. "On drums?"

"That's him," confirmed Holly, as the kid waved happily to us between pounding the drums. "I have a soft spot for Dave since we kidnapped him, and now that he's given up on a life of crime,

I asked the band here if Dave could audition to play a few songs. He's also going to work part-time in one of Howard's trucking warehouses to save up for college."

I spent a few minutes updating John on the details of what he'd missed during his trip, glossing over the part about taking Dave against his will to Florida.

"Hello everyone," said Gerda, walking in. She was wearing the black BCBG jumpsuit that Sophie had forced her to buy last summer, and incongruously, she had a happy expression on her face that came as close as she ever does to smiling. "I have big news."

"Gerda, you look almost cheerful," said Holly. "I'm worried."

"I reach an agreement with Eula this afternoon to purchase her cottage," said Gerda. "And in weird development, Eula herself is going to buy the house of Mariellen Merriwether, which Lilly Merriwether has decided has too many bad memories for her to keep. Eula did say she plans to spend most of her time sailing the world and maybe buy condo somewhere warm, so we probably not gonna see too much of her around town."

"That's the holiday gift that keeps on giving!" said Holly. "Oh, hi again, Eula," she added, as the girl in question suddenly popped up next to Gerda. "Congratulations on your new home on Camellia Lane. I'm sure you won't be as miserable there as Mrs. Merriwether was."

"Are you going to redecorate?" asked Bootsie. "Because all the pink is cheerful, but who knows if that contributed to the Merriwether mental state?"

"I'll probably install a fabulous new kitchen." Eula shrugged dispiritedly. "And turn the barn into a gorgeous sculpture and painting studio. But I can't help thinking this would have been the perfect place for me to share with a special man. If only Scooter and I hadn't split up!

"I've been doing a lot of landscape painting to take my mind off my heartbreak, but I can't stop thinking about how we would have been cruising to Venice in April, and how romantic it would have been with Scooter on a gondola," Eula added.

"Eula, the guy was engaged to another passenger who also had dreams of floating past the Doge's Palace with that shady lawyer-turned-scam artist. It wouldn't have been all that fun to fight over Scooter with Minnie Allington in a canal," Bootsie told her.

Seeing how downcast Eula looked, she added supportively, "And look how much better you're dressing these days. You'll probably find a new guy real quick!"

It was true that Eula had on a fabulous outfit, I thought to myself. She was actually wearing skinny black pants and a swingy silk top that looked great on her, and she still had her tan from the *Palace of the Seas*, which added a glowy look to her sour expression.

"Nice top," Joe told her, apparently less impressed than I was by Eula's stylish new vibe, and not extending the same compassion Bootsie had for Eula's heartbroken status. "Except once again, you've chosen to go French and flowy, when you'd be better off tailored and Tommy Hilfiger."

"I agree," seconded Gerda. "You are too short for this outfit," she told Eula. "However, please do not hold this opinion against me when we are finalizing the sale of your cottage."

"Well, I have something that will cheer you up. Eula, I want you to meet someone who's up from Florida and is an old friend of Mrs. Potts," said Holly. "This is Bingo Simmons, who happens to be your ex-boyfriend's half brother. Bingo's side of the family is the good half," she added. "He's nothing like Scooter."

We all exchanged hugs and greetings with Bingo, a really nice and super-mellow guy we'd met last year in Florida. Bingo inherited money, like Scooter, but is more the type of guy who likes to sit under a lemon tree in his backyard and strum a guitar than a scheming businessman. Most of the time, Bingo sleeps in a yurt (though said yurt is on his beautiful property in Magnolia Beach, alongside his fancy cottage and a pool).

"I want to apologize for Scooter," Bingo said, flashing a sweet smile at Eula, who looked like she was perking up a little.

"And since Scooter paid for his spot on the *Palace of the Seas* for the next four months, I'm going to be on the boat instead of him," he added.

"Really?" said Eula, her tiny face cheering up even more. "We'll be in Venice together?"

As Bingo and Eula headed for the bourbon bar, I gave Holly an admiring glance. "That was a nice thing to do," I told her.

"Bingo is way too sweet for Eula," she said with a shrug, "but I figure his thoughtful self might actually improve Eula. And if all goes according to plan, they'll get married and live in Magnolia Beach, where I'll only have to see Eula a maximum of one week per year!"

"YOU KNOW WHAT?" said Bootsie, looking at a group just outside the tent that included her husband, Will; Skipper the country club chef; Leena; Mrs. Potts; the Colketts; and Joe. "Howard's puffing on a cigar with that group out there. In fact, all of them, including Leena and Honey, are smoking Cohibas and toasting each other. I mean, I get that Howard's eating brisket, and he just found out he's getting his own cool shed with a moonshine still for Christmas, but he looks extra happy. Like, more happy than even brisket could make someone."

"That's probably because after he got home from Oregon last night and saw me eating a bowl of Rice Krispies, he knew something weird was going on, and we drove to the CVS at 1 a.m. to get the pregnancy test," Holly told us. "Which was positive!

"I'm excited of course, but I think Howard and Martha are more into this than I am. Anyway, we're going to need a bigger SUV that can accommodate a car seat for late-night takeouts and Restaurant Gianni dinners. I mean, Table 11 has room for one more tiny person, doesn't it?" she said.

After congratulations, hugs, and even a little tear in Gerda's eye, Sophie couldn't restrain herself. "I don't want to horn in on your awesome baby news," she said, "but I have news, too! Guess what Joe and I did today?" said Sophie, who looked fantastic in a strapless gold dress and matching heels. She jumped up and down a little and tapped her Pirate Red–painted toes in excitement, while for his part, Joe looked embarrassed.

"Um—booked your honeymoon, with a one-month cancellation policy in case your lawyers are wrong?" asked Bootsie.

"Did you start looking at how to exactly lay out tables in your backyard to accommodate seventy-eight wedding guests, like you were talking about before Thanksgiving?" Holly asked.

"We got my divorce papers signed by Barclay, which I then signed, took to my lawyers, and made official! My ex and I are officially split up!" shrieked Sophie. "And Joe and I got a wedding license!"

Since it turned out Officer Walt had become an officiant for his niece's wedding the previous summer, after another sip of bourbon, Joe told Sophie he thought it was time for their wedding.

Not in May or June in a garden designed by the Colketts, or in the hills of France, or on a beach in the Caribbean, but right then and there, in the tent filled with a Prince cover band, roses, and the delicious scent of brisket.

"We can move the roses into appropriate background for ceremony," said Gerda. "I do this right now."

"Is there a wedding tonight?" asked Nick from the donut shop, in his guise as Prince. "Because I think I have just the song for this."

Here, he grabbed the microphone, recited the opening lyrics of "Let's Go Crazy," and Dave and the rest of the band began playing along.

"Guys," said Officer Walt, waving the band to a halt, "you sound great, but let's do the wedding and then get to the music."

"I did have seven different Pinterest boards for wedding dresses and makeup, and then there were all the hors d'oeuvres ideas for a summer reception," said Sophie sadly. "If we get married right now, do you think I'll regret that I didn't get to use my wedding mood boards?"

"Sophie," Holly said, "look at Joe. You love him, right?"

"More than anything!" said Sophie, giving Joe, who looked pale and terrified, but determined, a little arm squeeze.

"Great," Holly told her. "I think it's time to walk down this aisle—well, across this dance floor to where Officer Walt is standing and where Gerda and the Colketts just formed a bank of red roses for the ceremony Who knows if Joe's ever going to want to enter into matrimony again?"

"Joe loves you, Sophie," John told her. "And the holidays is the perfect time to get serious about love," he added, smiling at me. "Which is exactly why I'm back home with Kristin," he added, taking my hand. I felt a glow inside, and it wasn't from the rum in the eggnog. This Christmas was going to be the best ever!

"Seize the moment, doll," Tim Colkett advised Sophie.

"You're so right!" shrieked Sophie. "Let's do this!" she said, as Nick started into the "*Dearly beloved*" part of the Prince song.

"And," she added happily, "Joe and I can always have that themed wedding reception this summer. And, a post-reception bachelorette weekend, and then there's the honeymoon, and some celebratory disco parties, and I can throw myself a shower. This is going to be great!"

About the Author

AMY KORMAN is a former senior editor and staff writer for *Philadelphia Magazine* and author of *Frommer's Guide to Philadelphia*. She has written for *Town & Country*, *House Beautiful*, *Men's Health*, and *Cosmopolitan*. She lives in Pennsylvania with her family and their basset hound. Her novels include *Killer WASPs*, *Killer Getaway*, and *Killer Punch*.